PRAISE FOR ANDREA HURTT

"COLORFUL, DESCRIPTIVE, FASCINATINGLY PROVOCATIVE... Andrea Hurtt's *Masquerade,* is a WONDERFUL story about relationships and consequences. Just when you think you know what happens next, you realize THAT YOU DON'T! Not by a long shot, because that's what deception is... a mind trick that lets you think you've got it all figured out. At least until everything unravels. This is a FANTASTIC first novel and I can't wait to see what stories Andrea Hurtt weaves next."

— DEB WHITE- STAFF WRITER FOR *NERDS AND BEYOND*

"*Maquerade* keeps you intrigued from the very first sentence. The writing is so descriptive I felt like I was right there, and when it ended I felt like I lived it! I eagerly await Andrea's next book!"

— DOROTHY CHAMBERLAIN

"A thrilling tale that pulls you into Grace's world. The passion, fear and blame that Andrea takes you through on this journey are so real that I found myself biting my nails through the last chapters. I can't wait to read more of her books."

— LINDA STECKER

"For the bibliophile who is looking for their next addiction, you have uncovered the secret of Andrea Hurtt's *'Maquerade'*! This stand-out novel weaves a suspenseful tale of love, deceit, and the necessity of discovering ones own strength and self worth. Her mastery of the pen and attention to detail is a fresh infusion of talent to the literary world and I cannot wait for the next edition!"

— RIANNA MELTON

MASQUERADE

ANDREA HURTT

PIECE OF PIE PUBLISHING

Piece Of Pie Publishing

11923 NE Sumner ST Ste 826515

Portland, OR 97220-9601

Cover by: MGDesigns

Editor: C.A. Szarek

For my Family

CHAPTER 1

"Maddie! Where's our Maddie?" the stage manager called for the star of the show, *her.*

As she stepped out onto the stage, enjoying the heat from the spotlight, Maddie took over. She fell in love with the boy-next-door her father had told her she could never have. While events unfolded, Maddie learned there was so much more out in the world.

The character went in search of something dangerous, something magical, only to discover she already had everything she desired in her own front yard.

Grace gave the performance of a lifetime—like she did at every single show.

She treated each performance as if it was the most important one of her life, because she never knew when it would be.

The cast took their applause and came back for the curtain call. The noise from the crowd was deafening.

If she did a thousand shows in her life, she'd still never get used to that sound. Her heart beat with the vibrations of the clapping. She felt so alive.

Her theater company was doing a US tour of their current

production, *The Splendids*. Their twelve-week run was almost over. They had two shows in Las Vegas, before finishing in Los Angeles.

She was so done with Vegas. Grace had stumbled during their last performance. Disappointed with herself for her screw up, she didn't want to go out with the cast at the end of the night to meet fans.

She headed back to the hotel, where she could be alone.

Grace plopped down on the middle of the bed she shared with Maxine, one of the contortionists, fighting with tears she didn't want to shed.

A bag of Reese's Pieces, her comfort food, was staring at her from on top of her suitcase, like it knew she needed to cheer herself up. She sprung up to get the sugary sweetness.

She curled up on the floor, resting her back against the foot of the bed, pulling her knees up to her chest.

A knock on the door jarred her out of her head. The sense of passing time eluded her, but the bag of candy resting between her ankles was almost empty.

Grace looked at the door. Who could that be? None of the girls she shared with ever knocked. "Yes?" She called from the floor, not wanting to move.

"Grace? Are you all right?" The voice was muffled through the door, but it was Charles, her handsome, yet young, costar.

Over the past five months, they'd gotten to be close friends. She had to kiss him twice a day during productions, but that hadn't changed their friendship.

"Hold on," Grace called, doing her best not to spill the last of her candy, when she stood. She failed, and little hard shells tumbled around. She jumped over them. At least she hadn't crushed them into the carpet. She took a deep breath, letting it out in a huff before she opened the door.

Charles stared, his brown eyes intense, his shoulders pulled back in arrogance. "Really, Gracie? You're gonna hang out in your room and pout because you tripped? It happens. No one can be graceful all the time."

She laughed with her friend, tension loosening in her shoulders. He knew, better than anyone, how *un*graceful she was.

The only time she pulled off the illusion was when she was on stage.

"Yes, I'm gonna pout. But you might as well come pout with me. You screwed up too."

He stepped into the room, but didn't see the spilled Reese's on the floor. *Crunch crunch* under the soles of his boots had Grace whirling around.

She shoved him out of the way. "Stop! You're ruining my candy!" She squatted down to scoop up the salvageable pieces, popping some of them into her mouth.

"Ick! Grace! That's wrong! It's been on the floor."

"It's Reese's. The five-second rule applies."

"I think it's been over five-seconds."

"I don't care." Grace jumped on the bed and grinned.

Charles sat on the edge of the mattress, putting his hand on her knee. "So, back to what you said a second ago, about me screwing up. What the hell? I am always perfect."

"My ass! You laughed when I tripped. It was so out of character. Louis would've run to Maddie's side. *Not* laughed at her!"

As hard as she tried to be mad, he was right.

It was silly of her to beat herself up over it. A misplaced cord had caused her to trip, not something *she'd* done.

"Well, if I screw up next week, which I am sure will, you're allowed to laugh at me. Fair enough?" His expression said he was serious.

"Why do you think you'll mess up next week? As you said, you're perfect."

Charles wasn't perfect. He was very much a screwball when not performing. Their rehearsals were always so much fun because he messed around half the time. However, much like

Grace; they let everything else go and allowed their characters to take over when they went on stage.

"My brother and some of his buddies are gonna be there."

"So?" she asked.

"So, I've always looked up to him. Like any little brother, all I've ever wanted was for him to be proud of me. This is my chance to show him what I've become, so I'm sure I'll screw it up." He smiled and patted her knee again before he ran that hand through his tousled blond hair. "I don't know which show he's coming to. He's busy, or so he says. But he guaranteed me he'd be at Saturday's Benefit Masquerade."

"Will you introduce me? I'd love to meet him."

"I guess. He's closer to your age. It still surprises me they got an old lady to play a teenager," he teased about their eight-year age difference.

"Old lady! Who're you calling an old lady?"

"You, of course."

She shoved at him, playfully, but hard, sending him crashing to the floor.

He landed with a great *humph*, followed by laughter.

Grace peered over the side of the bed.

He was still sitting on the floor. "Yeah, you and my brother will get along just fine. He likes to beat on me, too." Charles crawled back to the bed. "Everyone loves my brother." He sounded almost…sad. "Well, have a good one. I'd better go."

"Are you okay?"

"Yeah. Sure. See ya in the morning, Graceless," he called, and the door shut behind him.

♪♫

CHARLES and the entire production team arrived in Los Angeles on the Monday evening of their last week. They'd saved most of the company's marketing funds for this last hurrah.

The cast did multiple photoshoots, most of which were out in the hot California sun. They quickly learned a nice day wasn't conducive with full costumes and wigs.

"I think I'm about to lose this wig," Charles pointed out to the PR woman, standing off to the side, supervising.

"Agreed. Let's get you all out of costume."

That left normal street clothes as their only options. He had no problem switching from the khakis, white button up shirt, and brown vest that made his Louis costume and into his faded bluejeans and black sleeveless shirt. Now he was comfortable.

Grace, on the other-hand, appeared uneasy out of her costume. She crossed her arms below her chest, pulling the white off the shoulder shirt tight over her full breasts.

Charles looked on hungrily.

"They want to get a few of just you two," the photographer's assistant said, pulling Charles and Grace aside.

They followed to where there were a few dead tree trunks lying scattered about, the sun beginning to set behind them, scattering rays of pink and orange.

"I know you do this pose all the time," the photographer called. "But if you'll bear with me, Charles, can you please lift her. And Grace, don't forget to pop that left foot out behind you."

He had to hold back a grin as his hands slipped around her waist in a familiar pattern. But this time it felt different. More... personal.

"Charles, now go down on one knee, bend the other and put your foot on the ground."

He got down in the dirt, trying not to kick up more dust, positioned like a man in love about to propose.

"Sweetie," the photographer said, turning to Grace. "You're going to let him dip you back. Yes, like that. Now look into each other's eyes."

He stared into the depths of her blue-green orbs, loving how her long lashes fluttered as he held her gaze. There was nothing he wished for more, than to stare into her eyes forever.

"Grace," the photographer said. "I need you to look more in love, like your costar is doing."

What the man was asking for; it came naturally for Charles. Not because of his stellar acting skills either. He had been infatuated with this woman for over five months. Since the day they'd met.

The photographer kept moving around them, getting shots from different angles, reminding them to stay still.

Then he asked them to kiss.

"*What!?*" Grace asked.

Charles slid his left hand up from the nape of her neck, where he'd been holding her steady, into her beautiful chestnut hair. "It's okay," he encouraged, not taking his serious gaze off her. "We've been doing it everyday for five months. You kiss me in every show. Twice, actually."

Grace let out a small breath before putting one hand on his chest. "Yes, we do. But right now we aren't Maddie and Louis, we are Grace and Charles," she whispered, so only he could hear.

I know. The show is almost over and I can finally pursue you properly.

He leaned down, taking all the time in the world, allowing the photographer the opportunity to get good shots, and for the anticipation. He waited a lifetime to kiss *Grace* again.

This kiss *would* be different.

Stage kissing wasn't the same as normal everyday kissing; people's lips didn't completely touch. It was more like kissing just above or below the lips, never full contact, and certainly no tongue.

This time, Charles kissed her full-on.

He tried to part her soft cherry lips to further taste her, wanting more. The sweetness of her calling out to him.

Grace pushed at his chest to break away.

"Come on, Grace," he said in a breathy whisper. "We need to do this. It's important. It's to help promote the show."

"Like hell it is!" She tried to get out of his arms, but his fingers stayed entwined in her hair.

He would not let her go.

Charles gripped a little tighter and leaned close again, pressing their bodies together. He could feel the pounding of her heart against his hard chest. "Relax, Grace! Let's do this. It'll make some awesome pictures. You need this as much as I do."

"*Excuse m*e," was all she could get out.

His words came out exactly as he meant them, but not what he should've said to her. He quickly tried to recover.

"You know, the good press. You wanna get picked up by some movie production as much as I do."

"We can keep going *if* you kiss me the right way!" Grace snapped.

"I *was* kissing you the right way," he mumbled under his breath.

CHAPTER 2

GRACE STOOD IN THE SHOWER, LETTING ALL THE DUST, GRIME, AND emotions wash down the drain with hot water cascading over her tired body.

Charles was her dear friend, the one she'd always talked to about *anything*. Not this. He was the one she needed to talk about, not talk to.

How could he do that? Kiss me so... intimately?

Tonight was the benefit masquerade. She'd been looking forward to it all month, but after how things had gone at the photoshoot; all she wanted to do was spend the evening alone in the shower.

I know I have to go. Maybe it'll improve my mood. Besides, I don't have a choice.

The five hundred dollar per plate ticket went to helping fund children's theater programs in low-income areas. Part of the benefit was also a "dating auction".

The bidding started at one hundred dollars, and included one dance with the "date" and a photograph on the dance floor. Most of the female cast had volunteered to be auctioned off.

She hadn't volunteered.

She'd been drafted.

If it hadn't been for charity, she'd run for the hills.

She kept those kids in her mind, as she shut the water off and wrapped a towel around her body before stepping out.

Grace looked over at the gorgeous midnight-blue ball gown that hung from the door. It was supposed to make her feel like Cinderella.

Now she didn't even want to put it on, because it meant she'd have to face Charles again. Her emotions couldn't handle it.

Things would be different between them now, no doubt.

She'd only have to kiss him two more times.

Not that the unexpected kiss was bad; she'd felt his lips brush against hers so many times the past five months. She knew the softness of his lips like a lover, but that wasn't what they were.

It wasn't a shocker that something like this could happen; she'd seen it before in other companies. When actors were on the road with the same people for such a long time, in such intimate situations, relationships were bound to form.

Grace and Charles had a connection, a friendship she cherished. But nothing romantic. She'd put a stop to that the first week they met. Or so she'd thought.

Sometimes just one kiss could change everything. It could've sent them into a completely new type of relationship, overcoming the eight-year age difference. Or it could ruin their friendship forever, which was what she was afraid of.

She'd invited her best friend, Hope, to fly in from Washington and join her for the final two shows. Also, to the masked ball. She'd arrived that afternoon and they'd planned to get ready together.

As Grace slipped into her gown, all thoughts of her encounter with Charles fell away.

"Oh, Gracie! Your dress is breathtaking!" Hope said, stepping into Grace's hotel room. She held a huge garment bag in one hand, and a red rose in the other. She held it out for her dear friend. "This is for you!"

"Um, thanks? But you of all people know I don't like roses."

"I know, but it was sitting on the floor outside your door, so I assume it was for you."

Grace shook her head. "It's probably for one of my room-mates. Those girls have no clue how to do their hair or makeup, so they're at the theater having the team make them pretty. I'll... uh... leave it here for one of them." She set it in front of the TV, turning back to Hope.

"So, can you help zip me up?"

Grace's dress fell to the floor, hiding her beautiful silver strappy heels. She didn't care if she towered over Charles for the evening.

Hope pulled her gown from the huge garment bag and Grace gasped at the burgundy piece of art. It was stunning. With her chocolate hair in ringlets, she wanted to call her Scarlet.

"Well, dear Hope. You remind me of a character from my all-time favorite movie." They grabbed their masks from the desk in the bedroom and helped each other get the elastic over their heads without damaging their hair.

Hope had a burgundy mask with gold trim around the edging and glitter sprinkled across it.

Grace's mask was silver with matching trim around the edges and glitter filigree around the eyes. In the center was a diamond shaped midnight-blue stone that held two matching blue ostrich feathers in place.

They took one last look at themselves in the large mirrored closet doors and headed out into the night.

"Are you ready for this?" Grace asked. She grabbed Hope's hand and gave a gentle squeeze of reassurance.

The elevator seemed to be taking forever to get them down just a few floors.

Hope smiled. "I think I should ask you that. You look a little nervous. It's just like walking out on stage. If you need to be someone else tonight, that's okay, too."

How could she tell her it wasn't the crowd that concerned her, or even the chance she might trip over her own two feet, but seeing Charles would be too much?

She plastered on a smile. "I'm good. Let's do this!"

THE BALLROOM of the grand hotel was filled with women elegantly dressed in floor-length gowns and men in stunning black tuxedos. The décor was fascinating. It was as if they'd drenched the room in glitter.

A masked man came toward Grace and Hope. It was John, the fabulous sixty-year-old performer that played her father in the musical. Even with a mask on, there was no mistaking his shocking white hair. No matter how hard he tried to tame it, was always sticking in every direction. He reached for her hand and Grace accepted it. "Ah, my beautiful daughter," John said, before pulling her hand to his chest, just over his heart. "And who is this divine creature you have here?"

"I'd like you to meet my childhood friend, Hope. Actually, we met doing a small community play together."

"Oh? Another actress in my presence?"

"No, not me," Hope said. "I'm content to be behind the scenes or in a seat."

John took her friend's hand to graze her knuckles with a kiss. "Pity. You're as breathtaking as any diva I've ever seen on stage."

Hope was blushing; it was visible through her mask. She'd never been good at taking a compliment.

"If you'll please excuse me," John said. "It's time for a drink."

"Should we go get something as well?" Hope asked after the older actor had left them.

Grace smiled. "If you'd like a drink, I'll go over there with you, but I can't have one for another forty-eight hours. I've been alcohol-free for almost five months. No drinking while doing shows. But Sunday, after the last show, hell yeah."

"Oh, right. I forgot."

Grace insisted at least one of them should enjoy all the free liquor.

A ginger ale in her tall champagne glass, her smile faded. Her heart shot to her gut.

Charles was headed her way.

He wasn't alone.

Two other masked men trailed behind him.

A well-tailored tuxedo is to women what lingerie is to men.

She couldn't see the men's faces, but she still enjoyed the view.

Her costar stopped in front of her. The smile on his face was pure; her friend was back.

It made her heart soar. There were no signs of him being uncomfortable or any lingering regret. Maybe the kiss hadn't ruined everything. A great weight floated off her chest.

"Gracie, I want you to meet my brother, Nick, and his friend Blaze." His voice was suddenly harsh, belying his expression, as if he had to share his favorite toy.

His brother stepped forward.

Wow, he was tall, over six feet for sure. Even in her heels, Grace had to look up to him. She then glanced to his friend.

He was what Grace and Hope called a 'tall, dark, and handsome sex on a stick' kind of man. He had black hair, not too long, but enough he could run his fingers through it if agitated. It looked like it wanted to curl, but he must've had hair product on that was fighting against it, unsuccessfully. He wore a well-trimmed goatee. His mask was black with blood red trim.

She couldn't see the true color of his eyes, which were fixed on hers, but they were almost black. He had tattoos on his neck and hands and his fingernails were painted a glossy black.

He wasn't her type. Yet, Grace couldn't stop looking at him, intrigued by his gothic appearance. When he smiled, butterflies beat at her stomach and he had yet to say a word.

Blaze. The name suits him. He looks like he could destroy a woman's heart with one heated glance. Oh, the fire I bet he could bring.

"You must be Grace. Charles has spoken of you often and with such affection."

She tried to bring her attention back as her costar's brother spoke, but it was a struggle to take her eyes off Blaze.

The orchestra was playing, and it tripped her notice.

"May I have this dance?" Nick asked.

Charles stepped in between them. *"No."* His voice was sharp. "You're up for auction. You can't dance with anyone until then."

Grace hadn't heard that part of the arrangement, but his tone said it wasn't worth arguing over. "My apologies, but I must decline. I *am* up for auction, if you still want that dance. All the proceeds will help the children's theater."

Nick smiled again. "Well, then. See you at the auction."

"If you'll please excuse me." She nodded at Nick before glancing once more at his friend.

He was looking right back and their eyes locked.

Oh, dark brown, not black. Damn, His eyes are so... intense. Stop looking, Grace.

Hope bumped her shoulder playfully, bringing her attention back but it shifted to her costar and his movements.

Charles stepped up close to his brother. His voice was hushed low enough that no one else would hear, yet Grace didn't miss it.

"Do. Not. Buy. Her."

Nick's shoulders pulled back tight.

No doubt, he didn't like his baby brother telling him what he could and couldn't do.

Grace touched Hope's arm. "Let's move over that way. I should learn more about the auction, and I need to find out where you can be so you aren't standing alone while I go up there."

Her bestie laughed. "I'm a big girl; I can take care of myself."

Less than an hour later, Grace lined up with the other girls in the cast, about to be 'sold' to the highest bidder.

As she crossed the stage, her heart raced. She'd spent most of her days in the spotlight but *this* was different. Nerves gripped her insides, tightening her gut.

It worried her no one would buy her, but at the same time, that someone *would* and Charles would be less than courteous to the winner. Obviously, that kiss meant more to him than he let on.

She looked around to find Hope. Her friend was her rock. Grace found her standing close to Charles's brother, and Blaze.

The auctioneer started the bid for her at one hundred dollars.

Grace heard, rather than saw, Charles call out double that.

The bidding went on for what seemed like hours, the amount climbing. There were so many different male voices calling out, only one did she know.

Charles called out fifteen hundred dollars.

When the auctioneer called going once, going twice, another voice called out.

"Five thousand dollars!"

Her hands shook. She wasn't worth that much, even for charity. Who would do that?

She wasn't the only one with that thought. They scanned a spotlight through the crowd, trying to find the voice.

The winner held up his hand and the spotlight landed on Charles's big brother.

Her eyes found her costar, his face mottled red with anger. Grace had never seen anyone so furious before.

What the hell! He has no right to decide who I can dance with!

She glanced to Nick and his expression was smug; he was going to teach his brother a lesson.

CHAPTER 3

"That's your friend, right?" Blaze asked, glancing at Hope. "Things are going to get ugly now. Hold on tight."

The auction started and he called a bid of five hundred dollars. He was intrigued by Grace, recalling the way her eyes had lingered on him a moment longer than socially acceptable.

Blaze lifted his hand to rebid a one thousand. He lowered his arm when Nick grabbed his attention.

"Dude. She's mine."

"What? Why? I thought you wanted Scarlet."

"Didn't you see the way my brother was looking at her? He's totally fallen for his leading lady," his friend pointed out.

"So? Let him have her. You're not really interested, are you?"

"Not that I want to use the girl, but my little brother needs to learn a lesson. He's never been good with sharing. Even as kids, we'd fight all the time over stupid shit, even over whose toothpaste was whose. And it's obvious she has no interest in him. She was staring right at me."

"Wishful thinking, buddy. Not every girl has a thing for you."

"Five thousand dollars!" Nick yelled, instead of replying to his friend.

"Shit, man. Really?" Blaze shook his head. He didn't say anything else; his buddy walked away. He looked at Hope, to gauge if she had any clue of what was going on.

"Why is it always the blond that gets the girl?"

"I feel the same way, I mean, from our perspective. You know, it's always the blonde chick that gets the attention."

He laughed. "Yeah, I guess it's true. I've always had a thing for brunettes and redheads, myself. I don't think I have ever dated a blonde. Do you wanna dance?"

"Um, yeah. That would be nice, thank you."

Blaze offered his hand and led her to the back of the dance floor, where it was less crowded. "I've been looking forward to seeing this show. Even before Charles called Nick. Funny story... I wanted to grow up to be a magician."

"Really?" Hope asked.

"Yeah. Things didn't pan out in that department. Life took me a different direction. I read the show is getting national reviews. I'm sure part of it is because they have '*Charles Ford*.'" He said the name with a hint of disdain. "But it's the special effects of Der Hahn's magic that really got me wanting to come. I let Nick think he dragged me here. I'm glad he did."

He couldn't help but glance toward his friend and the lady he was so enchanted with.

"I hope Grace can sing as good as she looks," Blaze said under his breath.

"Well, I don't think they'd let her have the lead if she couldn't sing," Hope teased.

"Yeah, obviously. I just meant..."

His cheeks flushed with heat. He was grateful the mask would hide the redness that was likely there.

"That's why you were upset with Nick!" she exclaimed. "It wasn't about the money, it was about *Grace*! You're interested in her."

"I don't know what you're talking about."

"Yeah, okay Pinocchio," she teased.

To shut her up, he spun her out until their arms were outstretched. The momentum brought her twirling back to him and Hope laughed as he pulled her close to his hard chest, both their breathing ragged.

♪♫

THE AUCTION DUES had been paid and they matched most of the dates up.

Grace stood alone, last to be retrieved. She looked around.

Where's my date?

Charles approached her. He no longer looked angry, just sad. "I didn't want him to buy you because as soon as you're in his arms, you'll forget about me. Everyone loves my brother."

His youth was showing.

She felt the eight-year difference between them. Grace touched his cheek tenderly, something that had become a small piece of their friendship.

He put his hand over hers, as he looked into her eyes. "You know I'm in love with you, right?" he whispered.

"Charles—"

"There's my beautiful date," a man with a silky voice said.

Her friend whipped around to stare at his older brother. Brown eyes battled with blue. "She's not your date, Nick. You get one dance. Just remember that." He stormed away.

"Fun, isn't he?" big brother teased.

Grace narrowed her eyes. "Your brother has been a dear friend. Don't knock him like that."

"I'm sorry. I didn't mean to spoil anything. How about that dance?" He offered her the crook of his arm.

"I need to check on Hope first. She's all alone."

"Um, she's dancing with my friend, so it's all good."

She faked a smile and let him lead her to the dance floor.

Nick moved so smoothly and one dance led to another.

She found out although their relationship was strained, Charles spoke to his brother often, and *she* had been a major part of their discussions.

Discomfort swirled in her gut. She couldn't look him in the eye any more. Nick knew far too many intimate things about her.

She scanned the crowd for Hope and her burgundy dress. Her friend was still dancing with Blaze, clearly having more fun than she was.

Grace needed to get out of the uncomfortable situation. It was bad enough she was in the arms of a man whose brother said he was in love with her, but for him to know such private things about her was disconcerting. "Nick, I don't want to hurt your brother any further tonight. I have two more shows to do, so any chance I could get you to ask my friend Hope to dance?"

He chuckled. "Yeah. I should try and be more civil towards him. I think Blaze wouldn't mind dancing with a girl as lovely as you. Besides, your friend reminds me of a girl from a movie, so I gotta dance with her."

Grace giggled. "Yeah. I thought she looked like someone, too."

"Scarlet," they said together, then burst out laughing.

They moved closer to the couple, and Nick touched his friend's shoulder.

"Dude, switch me."

The smile on his friend's face said it all.

"Be careful, Grace. He's a little crazy," Hope teased.

She couldn't believe she was going from one awkward situation into another.

Nick offered his hand to Hope, and her friend accepted.

"So," Grace said to the dark-haired man.

Blaze slid his left hand along the side of her waist, until it rested on her lower back. He offered his right, and as soon as their hands touched, he pulled her against him.

She was so close, she could feel his heart beating against hers.

Then with no warning, he spun them around, her skirt swishing around their legs.

She had to laugh as she fought to breathe. She'd been worried he'd be a jerk, as Hope had tried to warn her, but he was such a gentleman.

"I don't think we were properly introduced," Blaze said, as he moved her around the dance floor.

"Charles said your name is Blaze?"

"Yes… *Grace.*"

Her name on his lips sent ripples through her body, tightening muscles in her abdomen.

How could his voice affect me like this? I feel it in my bones.

"So…" her voice failed. What's should she say?

He must've taken her hesitation as the right moment to change their positions.

Grace was expecting a step to the right, but he moved to the left, and she lost her footing. She almost fell, but Blaze caught her, sort of.

They both laughed when he misjudged the distance to her waist and his hands landed a little higher.

She turned eight shades of red but he grinned playfully.

"I meant to do that," he said with a sly smile.

"Well, then. I hope you enjoyed it." Grace was shocked she let that slip from her lips. It wasn't like her to be so crass.

"So, Grace. Tell me something about you, something your costars don't know."

"I love cats. But because of all the traveling, I can't have one."

Blaze pulled her in a little closer, their bodies pressing together. "I know what you mean. I am always on the road. Cats are great, but it's dogs for me."

Grace smiled. A new song began, and they continued to dance, no hint of separation. "My turn. Tell me something."

He licked his lip. "My favorite color's red, and I collect antiques. The older and more obscure, the better."

"Who told you?" she teased.

"Told me what?" he said, his expression showing his confusion with the quirk of one eyebrow.

"*My* favorite color is red and *I* collect antiques. Is someone playing a joke?"

"Seriously?" His dark eyes were wide, but sincere.

Grace nodded. Maybe it was a coincidence?

"My little apartment's full of stuff. My dining table and chairs are about a hundred and fifty years old. Solid oak. It'd take a sharp ax to even put a dent in one of the chairs."

They had so much in common, but not once did he mention the theater or acting. Grace had never fathomed being drawn to a man with makeup and tattoos, but there was something about Blaze that kept her in his arms, song after song. She kept wishing he would take his mask off; she really needed to see him. She needed to know what she was giving up by denying herself any type of relationship.

"MAY I CUT IN? Just one dance." John stood beside them, holding his hand out to Grace.

Blaze reluctantly let her go. "Grace, thank you. I hope I get the pleasure of dancing with you again this evening." He bowed regally to her and walked away, leaving her standing there with the man that played her father.

After John danced with her, they whirled her around from one man to another.

Most of the faces she recognized as either cast or crew, but there were a few older gentlemen she had the pleasure to dance with that had the possibility of being benefactors to the theater company.

"Why should I invest in this company?" one man asked as he swayed her back and forth in just one spot.

"Why would you *not*? No one can compare to the visionary

that is Jason. Just wait until you see the show tomorrow. If you're not completely in awe when the curtain closes, I'll hang up my dancing shoes and walk away."

The gentleman grinned ear to ear. "You are *that* sure, that you'd wager your career?"

"I would."

It was hard to focus on impressing these men, when all Grace wanted was to find Blaze again. However, the money bags needed to be wooed, and John had said it was up to her.

It seemed like hours before they finally allowed Grace to walk away. She found Hope, but there was no sign of her tall, dark man.

Damn, things were just getting interesting with Blaze. No! Don't think like that. It's better if I never see him again.

CHAPTER 4

CHARLES SAT IN SILENCE WITH HOPE ALONG A PLANTER BOX FULL of flowers and plants that looked like elephant ears. How did his night ended up as it had? Nothing had gone right for him. This was supposed to be a night he'd never forget.

It would be.

Not the way he'd wanted.

From the moment his big brother and his friend had arrived, he'd known it would be a hell of a night.

Nick had stared at *his* woman with lustful eyes.

It was Charles' own damn fault.

If he hadn't spent so many hours the past five months on the phone with his brother, telling him all about Grace's beauty, her caring soul, and how he wanted her more than anything, Nick wouldn't be looking at her the way he was.

Shit, Nick. Why does everything have to be a fucking competition with you?

He should've known how things would go.

His brother never changed.

Charles had tried to clearly point out to his brother, Grace was the one woman he needed to stay clear of. His words fell on deaf ears.

When the auction started, he anticipated having trouble with his brother. Rightly so. Nick had continued to outbid him every time he'd raised his hand.

A voice, not his brother, yet one he'd known since he was a small child, had called out a bid.

He glared at Blaze with burning eyes.

It was bad enough he had to fight his brother for the right to have Grace for the night, but now Blaze was joining in.

He'd never had a beef with the man before. As his brother's best friend, he'd seen the best and the worst of Charles and usually stood by him when Nick was cruel or unkind. The thought of Blaze touching Grace gave him murderous thoughts.

Nick had cut him off at his last bid, calling out an astronomical amount, essentially ending the bidding war.

He could feel the anger burning through him, heating not only his cheeks but his ears.

Charles had lost the chance to spend the night with Grace wrapped in his arms. He'd had to remind himself it was only one night.

Soon enough he'd have *every* night to spend with her.

When he saw what he assumed was happiness for being bought by his brother written on her face, it spurred him on.

He needed to tell her right then he loved her. It couldn't wait another night, or he might lose her forever to his brother's charm.

Of course his brother had taken that special moment away from him, too.

He watched as Grace danced with Nick for more than the one allotted song. His hands had turned white from the constant tightening of his fists.

He'd had to stay calm or he would do something he'd regret.

For all their issues, the many times they had fought, both

verbally and physically, not once had they thrown punches in public. Charles was about to make an exception.

He was grateful when Maxine, his favorite contortionist, asked him to dance. It took his mind off beating his brother and essentially killing his own career.

After one dance, he'd been whisked from one lady to the next.

Each time he tried to find Grace, he saw only Nick. Half the time he couldn't see whom his brother was with, there were too many bodies on the dance floor between them.

It didn't help his anger.

When he finally spotted her, she was swaying back and forth ridiculously with a much older, balding man. Surely one of the possible benefactors Jason wanted them to woo.

So many times he got so close to her, reaching to grab her attention for a dance, and he got pulled away. For every rich old man at the event, there seemed to be a hungry wife, reaching for him, pulling him to the dance floor to press their wrinkled cheeks against his hard chest.

It irritated him.

He had to woo them. It was his job that evening, as Jason had drilled into him before heading over to the ballroom earlier that evening.

He wanted to get away.

More than an hour had passed and she was still flitting from one man to another, Charles keeping a watchful eye on her. Just in case she needed him. He kept hoping for a handsy man he could valiantly rescue her from, but to his disappointment, everyone was courteous.

Finally getting a break from dancing around one a.m., he took a moment to grab another glass of champagne.

He stood off to the side, hiding in the shadows, scouring the sea of tuxedos for his brother, or Blaze.

Charles found Nick, just walking off the dance floor, Grace's petite friend on his arm. He set down his now empty glass and headed straight toward them. "I see you finally got a clue about Grace." He stepped up to them, his voice sharp with contentment.

"No, I just found someone I liked more. But fear not, I think you still have competition, little brother." Nick didn't explain further. He excused himself to Hope. "Blaze and I really need to be going. We have another event to go to tomorrow before the show. Perhaps I'll see you again." He walked away, leaving Hope alone with Charles.

Charles studied the woman standing beside him.

She was definitely *not* his brother's type. Everyone knew the saying, 'opposites attract', but he'd never believed it to be true in real life.

He didn't care if Nick liked her or not, at least his brother wasn't pursuing Grace further.

Nick had left her here with him, so she was fair game for retaliation.

He gave her his million watt smile. There was only one woman who was able to resist his charms. His Grace.

In the meantime, he'd use this friend of hers to his advantage. "I'm sorry. I don't think I ever got your name." Charles offered his hand.

"Hope."

He brought her hand to his lips and pressed a tender kiss to her knuckles. He looked up into her chocolate eyes and smiled. "Why is a lady as beautiful as you, spending time with an asshole like my brother?"

"I, um…" She seemed to struggle with her reply. "Hey, my feet are killing me. Do you mind if we sit?" Hope glanced over at the white granite tile planter box.

He followed her gaze. The wide top would work as a 'seat'.

Charles led her over and sat on her left side, and her skirts filled the space between them.

She smiled. "Thank you. I'd hate to be sitting here all alone, waiting for Grace."

His shoulders slumped forward, he lost his perfect posture. He wanted to get back at his brother, and using this woman would be the easiest way.

But... she had such a kind smile and was Grace's friend. He couldn't hurt her to get even with Nick.

"I love my brother but sometimes he can be such an ass. He kept Grace all to himself, and I haven't had a chance to dance with her."

"Actually, it was me he spent most of the night with," she whispered.

He took a deep breath and let it out in a sigh. All he could see was Nick laughing with Grace as he spun her around the dance floor, her beautiful blue gown billowing out around her shapely legs as she turned in circles.

Why couldn't it have been me she danced with, laughed with? I want to dance with Grace. All I ever get is Maddie. I want her soul, not just her body.

He envisioned asking Hope about her relationship with Grace, when she broke through his thoughts.

"So, tell me a little about you. When I was dancing with Blaze he was saying the musical was popular because of you. Why is that?"

I don't want to talk about me.

Charles stuck his thumbs into the edge of the pockets in his slacks, to stop from making fists again. His therapist had been trying to break him of that habit, unsuccessfully.

The best way to get her to talk about Grace, was probably to give her what she wanted. Talk a little about himself, then a little about her... and Grace.

"I've been a pop star since I was about twelve. I've sold over one million albums. A few years ago, I dated some rather popular Hollywood girls, all blondes. That landed me in the spotlight, but not in a good way. I'm done with blondes."

"So why are you doing an off-Broadway play instead of movies or something?"

"I wanted to try something different. I don't like being told what I should do..."

His words came to a halt .

Grace was slowly gliding their way.

Finally, what he'd been waiting for all night was standing before him.

Then Hope spoke, shattering the illusion he was visioning; Grace wrapped in his arms, laughing with him as he glided her across the dance floor.

"Are you about ready to go? I'm sure your feet are killing you in those shoes."

"You can't leave. I haven't had a dance yet," Charles protested, jumping up from his seat on the planter box.

Grace scoffed. "Charles, we dance together every day. My feet hurt, and I've danced all night."

"Please," he begged. He didn't want to give up so easily, but one thing he'd learned the past five months, never push her too far.

"Okay, fine. As long as I can take my shoes off first."

He offered his hand so she could bend over and accomplish her task.

"Hope?" she asked.

Hope took her pumps. "Don't worry about me. Just keep it to one song, please?"

Charles held his breath as he moved them back inside. And to the hardwood of the dance floor.

He wrapped his hand around her waist, feeling the heat of her skin through the dress.

They danced in silence for a while.

He tired to keep eye contact but she kept looking away. He tensed as his anger slowly built.

"Charles, is everything all right?" she whispered in his ear when he pulled her in closer to him.

"You know it's not."

"Because of the way your brother acted?" Grace leaned back to look at him.

"That's part of it. But I knew that would happen," he pointed out.

"What would happen?"

"You falling for my brother," he said. He was accusing her now, his brows drawn tight.

"Damn it, Charles. Did you not see I only danced with him a few times? I danced with half the damn room while I was at it! I have no interest in falling for him, or *anyone*!"

They'd stopped their slow rotation and were now still.

"I'm not doing this tonight. We have two more shows we need to get through." She dropped his hand and walked away, leaving him standing alone on the dance floor.

CHAPTER 5

HOPE AND GRACE SAT ON THE BED, THEIR DRESSES UNZIPPED BUT still pooled around them. They'd gone to Hope's room, rather than Grace's shared room so she had nothing to put on and sitting on the bed in a tight dress was uncomfortable. She had begged her bestie to spill on the evening. They both got comfortable in their nests of fabric and started to dish.

"I was a little nervous standing next to the two hottest men in the room. You've always been the outgoing one, not me. I had no idea what to say! But Blaze, oh my! A girl could get lost in those dark eyes," Hope said.

Grace tried to hide her smile. "Tell me about it."

"I think he's interested in you."

"What? No," she denied, even though the notion made her heart race.

"Didn't you see him bidding for you? Nick shut him down though! I don't understand why he gave up that easy, not when he kept bringing all our conversations back to you."

"He did?"

"Yeah. You should have heard him when Nick said he was just doing it to teach his brother a lesson. A very *expensive* lesson."

What could Grace say to that? On one hand she was thrilled this man was as curious about her as she was of him. At the same time, she was torn.

Aside from denying herself liquor during a production, she also refused to get involved with anyone. She'd shut Charles and his advances down the first week they'd met. She'd have to do the same now.

"I know the money goes to the charity, but that pisses me off that Nick *used* me like that. I get it, he has issues with his brother, but that was a dick move."

"Why, Gracie! Did you just use foul language?" her friend teased.

"That wasn't foul."

"For you, it was!"

They both burst into a fit of schoolgirl like giggles.

Gasping for breath, Hope directed the conversation back to Blaze, who Grace didn't want to talk or think about.

"But in all seriousness, Grace. Maybe you should consider it's time to open your heart again. You can't keep it closed forever. Blaze could be exactly what you need."

"I don't need a man in my life right now. I have you."

"And you'll always have me. There's room for more you know."

"I know. I'm just not ready yet."

Would she ever be?

WELL AFTER THREE AM, Grace snuck into her room, trying to be as quiet as possible.

Please, let the others be out cold. I just want to go to bed and sleep for days.

She set her mask on the nightstand and hurried to the bathroom. After her gown was back in the garment bag, and her face washed clean, she crawled into bed, ready for sleep to claim her.

. . .

"MAY I HAVE THIS DANCE?" She could feel his voice resonating through her, vibrating through her bones. It was deep and sensual.

He was wearing a mask, and all she could see was black eyes.

Grace couldn't answer him; she seemed to have no voice. So, she nodded.

He offered her his hand.

The warmth of him spread through her entire body; she could feel the heat in places she wouldn't have expected.

He pulled her closer.

Grace could now see his eyes were not black, just a dark brown.

He leaned into her, his breath spilling across her face.

She held her own and closed her eyes.

Please, don't stop. Closer, come a little closer.

He pulled away from her.

No.

She opened her eyes to look at him again.

His eyes were no longer dark brown, they were golden. She tried to take away his mask to see why his eyes changed.

Grace pulled it up and over his head. What was wrong with his black hair? It was blond.

No!

GRACE BOLTED UPRIGHT and wide awake, her hand going reflexively to her throat. She was so tired but didn't want to go back to sleep and see Charles's face again.

The kiss *had* changed everything. Not for the better.

"How am I going to make it through the next two days?" She glanced around the small hotel room, worried her sudden outburst had woken her roommates. Even in the dark of the night she could see the bodies in the bed beside hers were unmoving. She laid back down and listened to Maxine's soft breathing, envious she couldn't fall asleep.

She loved Charles; he was one of her dearest friends. That

was all they'd ever be.

He needed to understand that.

Grace reached for her phone on the nightstand and disconnected it from the charging cord.

She knocked her mask to the floor in the process, but didn't bother to pick it up. Grace shoved the phone and her head under the covers to find her tunes. She had a 'sleepytime' playlist for occasions like this. Mostly soothing piano tunes, but there were classical pieces with full orchestra.

She turned the volume to the lowest level, tucked the phone under her pillow, and tried to fall back asleep.

"WHERE IS EVERYONE?"

Grace could hear the orchestra but she was standing alone, in the middle of the ballroom. She looked down to lift her full skirt up to see her bare feet. "I love the feel of the wooden floor against my skin."

She spread her arms wide, threw her head back to spin 'round and 'round, her skirt billowing around her. She laughed, the sound filling the space, almost blocking out the music.

Grace stopped when someone touched her waist. She was afraid to look at his eyes, so she glanced at his lips.

He ran the tip of his tongue across to moisten them.

She bit her bottom lip, the pressure throbbing back under her teeth.

"If you don't stop biting your lip, I'll have to stop you."

The voice was familiar, but she was still afraid to look at him. She looked away.

He brought a hand to her cheek to turn her back to him.

She still kept her eyes on his lips.

He slowly moved in toward her, one inch at a time. He tilted his head to the left as he got closer.

Grace couldn't take her eyes off him, afraid if she closed her eyes he might disappear, or change.

Their lips met, and his were soft like rose petals.

He gently parted her mouth and their tongues collided, a sweet dance together.

As they kissed, his warm hands slide around her waist, pulling their bodies so close. She could feel his heart beating, her own trying to match his. Her heart was beating so much faster; she couldn't get it to slow.

Their kiss broke, they both need to breathe.

Grace could feel his fingers on the back of her dress.

Is he pulling at the zipper? I don't care. This dress is too tight anyway.

She reached for his mask as he worked her zipper lower.

He quickly, but gently pushed her hands away and shook his head.

Air rushed her bare skin, as her dress fluttered to the floor.

Where are my bra and panties?

She was standing before this dark man with nothing on but her mask.

"If I'm going to be naked, I should be completely naked." Grace pulled the mask off her face and let it fall to the floor, landing on her gown.

He offered her his hand and she stepped out of the fabric.

She peeled the jacket off his body and let it drop.

Her companion stepped around her, so her back was to him now.

His warm lips touched her left shoulder and his hands snaked around to land on the lower half of her torso. His fingers slid up and down her stomach, splaying out then pulling in, teasing her skin, all while he delivered soft, hot kisses along her shoulders and neck.

Grace's body was going up in flames. She tried to turn in his arms; she was ready to look at his eyes. She wanted to watch him watch her as he filled her body with fire.

He wouldn't let her turn. His hands explored lower, she didn't think she could stay standing much longer.

She could feel something building within her; she was sure her body was going to explode.

Her knees were weak and he lowered her to the floor, still not facing her. She was on her knees, her back pressed against his chest, using her gown to cushion her.

She couldn't take it, she needed to see him.

She pivoted on her knees to face him.

He pushed her back onto to her gown and she could hear and feel the crunching of her mask beneath her. He leaned down, putting his hands on either side of her head. "Grace, do you want this?" he asked, his voice husky.

"Yes," she whispered.

"GRACE, damn it. Get up! Do you still want this?"

She opened her eyes, the sun spilling into the room. Maxine stood beside the bed, holding her mask.

It was crushed.

She sat up so fast it made her dizzy.

"I didn't see it on the floor, and I think I stepped on it. I'm sorry."

The girl tossed the mask on the bed, fake apology written across her face.

Some of the girls in the company were jealous of her interactions with Charles, like it was her fault she'd gotten the lead role. She glared back at her roommate before turning to assess the damage.

Grace picked up the mask, running her fingers lovingly over the midnight blue feathers, her body still vibrating from the oh-so-real-dream she'd just encountered.

Blaze? Had he been the man in my dreams?

"Oh, yeah," Maxine stood in the doorway as she and the other two actresses were heading out the door. "There's a rose in the bathroom for you." The door slammed closed behind them.

Grace crawled out of bed and headed for the bathroom. There, on the top of her makeup case was a red rose.

She stared, confused. Was this the same rose Hope had

brought in the night before? She peeked out the bathroom door and her pulse speed up. The rose was still sitting in front of the TV. She picked the flower up off her makeup case and placed it with the other rose.

When she returned to the bathroom, she stared at herself in the mirror. She had bags under her eyes. "Pete will be furious with me."

Their head makeup artist hated when he had to cover things like sleepless nights and hangovers.

"Maybe a hot shower will help?" She was usually one of the first to arrive at the theater on a performance night, but this time, she waited as long as she could.

When she got there, she headed straight to the women's dressing room.

Not that they didn't go into each other's rooms all the time, but Charles wouldn't start a confrontation in front of all the girls.

Half the female cast, and a few of the guys want you, Charles. Why can't you see I don't?

He was good-looking, had a rock hard body and a few tattoos aside; he had a dynamic personality.

She'd been surprised when she'd found out he was single. She'd told him from the very first day; she wanted nothing more than a working relationship. It'd blossomed into a friendship she hadn't known she'd wanted.

Grace made it through the pre-show work up without even seeing him. As curtain call got closer, she worried. It wasn't like him to miss huddle.

"Grace, stop fretting," John said as she played nervously with a ringlet from her wig.

Tonight was their first L.A. show. She had to continue wooing the potential benefactors from the night before.

Hope was also out there, and Blaze.

Her head swam at the idea of finally seeing him without the mask.

Stop it, Grace. It's better to not *see what you can't have.*

Five minutes to curtain, Charles appeared.

He headed straight for her, and for once in the past twenty-four hours, she was happy to see him.

Grace opened her arms and he walked right into her embrace.

He brought his lips so close to her ear; she could feel the heat of his breath.

"I'm sorry, Gracie. I should've waited until tomorrow night to tell you how I feel. How I have always felt. It was wrong of me to stress you out right before our most important performances. Will you forgive me?"

She pulled back and smiled. "Can we talk about this after the show?" She was trying to be sweet and they were about to go on stage

He stepped back, as if she'd slapped him, and glared. "Can't you just forgive me so we can move on?"

"I forgive you, Charles, but I still think there are things we need to talk about." Grace reached to touch his cheek like she always did when he was upset about something.

The look in his eyes told her what she'd failed to see.

Grace had inadvertently led him on.

What she saw as comfort and friendship, *he* took as flirting and love.

Her heart wretched.

"Charles, I'm the one who should ask for *your* apology."

She didn't get to explain further; they were pulled in opposite directions for the curtain call.

GRACE HAD NEVER BEEN one for scanning the audience, especially in a theater this big, but she caught herself on more than one occasion looking out, trying to locate Hope and Blaze.

She knew better than to look out into the crowd.

Grace was Maddie after all, and *her* entire world was on stage, not out in the crowd.

The show reached a scene in the field, where Maddie and Louis meet up. Charles broke character.

When they were about to have their quick lip-touch, Charles whispered, "I love you."

Only Grace could hear him, but it wasn't Louis's line.

It was all Charles.

The kiss that was supposed to be a peck, was like the kiss in the desert.

It was too real and too long.

Because she was on stage, there was nothing Grace could do. She had to stay as Maddie, who was in love with Louis.

This would further complicate things.

The crowd cheered and they continued their song.

When the song ended, Maddie was kidnapped and dragged off the stage.

Grace watched from the curtains as Louis fought the roustabouts off.

She was soon brought back on stage and the scene continued.

Focus! You are Maddie. You can't be angry right now!

IT WAS QUITE a while until they were both off stage together.

Charles came backstage, and they only had about two minutes until their next entrance.

This was the only chance she had to clear things up.

She grabbed his arm and moved him away from the curtain, and as close to the outside wall as she could. "Charles."

She didn't get to finish.

He pulled her to him, turned their bodies, and pressed her back up against the wall. Then his mouth assaulted hers.

Grace tried pushing hard on his chest to get him to stop.

When it didn't work, she went limp.

Charles pulled away from her, just enough to see her face. His eyebrows were furrowed in anger; his eyes dark with rage. "I thought you wanted me to kiss you. You were more than willing on stage."

"No, I wasn't. That was so wrong of you! To break character for your own gain! How is that right? I wasn't kissing you back; Maddie was kissing Louis! And it was supposed to be a peck, not a full kiss!" Grace took a deep breath. "Charles, I love you. I hope you know that. But I love you like..."

"Don't say a brother, anything but that."

"Please, don't do this. You don't love me, it's just residual feelings from Louis and Maddie. I just want my friend back." She whispered the last line. Grace slipped out from under his arm and moved to the other side of the stage.

She was so grateful they had different entry points for the next and final scene.

Grace took a few deep breaths and allow Maddie to take over. She left everything behind the curtain as she entered Maddie's world again.

As the final scene began, she lost a little bit of Maddie, the emotions coming from Grace.

Maddie's words were exactly what Grace needed to say.

She only hoped Charles could see it was from her, too.

"I'm sorry, Louis."

"Don't be. You were right. I was being unreasonable."

"What about what I did? I was wrong, too."

They sang their last song; *There For Me* and Grace could see a difference in Charles.

"I've missed you, Louis," Maddie and Grace whispered.

"I've missed you, too."

"You're hurt. Let me see if I can help with that."

She reached for his cheek but he caught her hand. The metaphor was so clear in her words. "You did already."

He brought his hands to her face. "You were damaged, too."

They were silent for a moment.

"Oh! It's snowing."

He took his coat off and wrapped her in it.

She smiled. "I think we could both fit in here," she said, offering to let him in.

His hands were on her cheeks again and she closed her eyes as he kissed her eyelids.

She looked at his eyes and they were more golden now.

Grace saw her friend again.

CHAPTER 6

"Is this seat taken?" Blaze asked the brunette sitting alone in the seat next to his ticket, Nick trailing behind him.

"Um, no," was all she could get out.

"I know it's odd but would you mind sliding over one seat and sitting in between us? I want to ask you a few questions about Grace, if you don't mind?"

She stood up; they did a little dance, switching places.

He tried to ease into his inquiry with a simple question. "Have you seen the show before?" When she didn't answer, he was afraid he's get nothing beneficial out of her. "You know, it's okay for you to talk once in a while."

Before she could answer, the curtains opened.

The show was amazing.

Blaze could feel the torment the characters were going through, the emotions so intense he could've sworn they were real. He could see why Charles had fallen for his leading lady.

Her talents were impressive. That *boy* could never handle a woman like her. He'd known Chuck since he was about ten and he hadn't really grown up yet.

When the curtain call ended and his view of Grace eliminated, he looked at Hope, not ready to give up on interrogating her.

"You are staying for the cheese and wine tasting, right?" Nick interrupted.

"Wine?"

"Dude, you're an idiot. Didn't you see the sign when we came in? They're hosting a cheese and wine party to raise money for the company. Damn, pay attention."

Hope reached over and touched his shoulder.

"Of course I'm going. Grace is my best friend and I'm here to support her."

"Then may I offer you my arm and escort you?"

"I would be de—" She didn't get to finish the sentence because Nick came up to the other side of her and offered his arm without asking.

Blaze tried not to be irritated with his friend. He wasn't hitting on the girl; he only needed information. "I really want you to tell me a little bit about her. The sooner the better," he whispered right above her ear.

♪♫

GRACE SMILED to herself to see Hope, her arms locked with both men. When they were just a few feet away, she dared glanced over at Blaze.

Their eyes locked for the briefest moment, and Grace had to break away. She made the mistake of looking at his lips. Her cheeks flushed with heat, and it spread down her body, as she remembered the dream of him the night before, when he'd taken over her body on the ballroom floor.

The way he smiled at her made her feel like he could read her mind. Like somehow he knew about the dream.

She bit her lower lip, hoping the pain would scatter her thoughts and erase the images.

Hope broke contact with the two men and enfolded Grace into a tight embrace. "What a fabulous show, Gracie, I think this was the best one yet."

"Thank you. I was really into character." She didn't elaborate. Especially since Charles's brother was right there and he was sure to know what was going on.

Nick extended his hand.

Grace outstretched her hand, expecting a shake.

Instead, he brushed his lips gently across her knuckles. "Impressive, Grace. I was almost brought to tears at the end. It was a very emotional scene. Even my brother poured everything into it."

She could hear the undertone of his words.

Oh, God.

He noticed what had gone on, onstage.

Did anyone else?

Nick turned to Hope. "Would you like to join me for a drink?"

Her bestie accepted and they went to the cash bar, leaving Grace alone with Blaze.

Her insides folded into knots as she gazed at his beautiful face for the first time. She studied his eyes to his facial hair and everything in between.

His eyes are like milk chocolate tonight. I could've sworn they were dark brown last night.

His lips caught her off guard. Grace couldn't recall staring at them the night before, but after the dream she had, she could've sworn she knew them intimately.

She was burning up. Heat brushed her neck and rushed her cheeks all over again. She caught herself biting her lower lip once more.

He touched her chin and gently pulled down. "You shouldn't bite your lip," he said. "It makes you look like you need to be kissed."

If Grace imploded before, she certainly was in danger of it

now. She needed to change the subject. "So Blaze, what do you do for a living?"

"I'm in the entertainment industry," he said.

"Oh my God, I knew it. You're a porn star. All the good guys are either gay, married, or porn stars." She was teasing of course, but had made her voice sound serious.

Blaze laughed so hard, he might've fallen over.

Nick put his hand on his friend's shoulder. He and Hope had rejoined them. "What is so funny?"

Blaze appeared to be having a hard time catching his breath; his face was all red and he was panting through his chuckles. "Dude, she thinks we're porn stars!"

Hope giggled.

"No really, Blaze. What you do for a living?" Grace asked.

He smiled big, the light reaching his eyes. "I am in the entertainment industry. I'm a stage performer."

Grace had had enough of his vagueness. She was a stage performer, too. When someone asked her what she did for a living, she explained she was an off-Broadway actor.

He needed to be a little more specific, or she would walk away to teach him a lesson.

"I'm sure you already know who I am. So let's quit playing games," Blaze said. His face darkened, and his statement was serious with a side of accusation.

Grace reared back.

What the hell?

Know who he was?

"I'm sorry, Blaze. I don't know who you are, other than a friend of Charles's brother. So yes, let's quit playing games."

He wore obvious shock, his mouth hanging slack. No one spoke and tension rose in the silence.

Nick stepped up to the plate. "I'm surprised my brother hasn't told you all about us. You know he has a musical background, correct?"

"Yes," Grace snapped. "I knew one of his songs when it first came out. I think it was called *'Beat Back'*?"

"Yeah, that's right. But did you know he had an older brother in a pop band?"

Maybe Charles had mentioned something before, but she had no interest in his family life.

"So you have heard of us, then? *Razor's Edge...*"

Grace shook her head. It couldn't be them. She had to play it cool as her hands shook. "I don't keep up with the music scene. I mean, there's a few songs I love, I'll catch on the radio once in a while or on a playlist, but I don't follow bands."

Hope leaned into her. "You know that song you like, *Unfinished*? I think that's them."

"Are you sure?"

Her friend nodded. She pulled out her phone and Googled the song. The results showed the artist was *Razor's Edge*.

"Okay, all that proves is the name of the band was right. That doesn't mean *they're* part," Grace teased to hide her discomfort.

Nick and Blaze nodded at each other and sang.

> "Pretending You were never here, Stuck in a world
>   of dreams,
> Wishing I could heal my heart, All I do is scream,
> Without you I am, Unfinished."

GRACE RECOGNIZED THOSE VOICES. *Unfinished* was one of her favorite songs. They were singing to *her*, sending pleasant vibrations through her body. She didn't like the feeling. She'd just discovered a voice that'd calmed her rough nights belonged to one of the men standing before her.

He was handsome, dark and dangerous; and she needed to have nothing to do with him.

Back away, Grace. If ever you were to let a man into your heart again, it shouldn't be this one. He will destroy you.

"That's cool. So what are you drinking tonight?" she asked Hope, trying to quickly change the subject.

Blaze scoffed. "*That's cool?* We tell you we're part of the number one pop band in the world and all you can say is '*that's cool*'?"

Was he being silly or he was seriously upset? It didn't matter. She couldn't get any closer to this man. She needed to get away fast before she did something she would regret for the rest of her life.

"Not to insult you or anything, Blaze, but yeah, *that's cool*. It doesn't change anything. You're still that the nice dark-eyed guy I danced with last night. Would you prefer I fawn all over you?"

"Hey, Grace, can I talk to you for a sec?" Victor, another actor in the play tugged her elbow.

She jumped at his appearance and plastered on a smile. "Uh, sure."

Blaze didn't get a chance to reply to her snarky comment.

GRACE WALKED AWAY with the other man.

Blaze hadn't meant to offend her; he was use to women knowing who he was, and wanting him for that reason.

She was different.

"I promise she's normally not this snarky. She's just been a little stressed out. If you give her another chance…" Hope voice jarred him.

"Actually, I find it quite refreshing. Because of my bad-boy appearance and attitude, people have a tendency to avoid confrontation with me. She's a little spitfire. She kind of reminds me of my Nana." He cocked his head to the side. "There is one thing I don't get."

"What's that," Hope asked.

"Not to sound cocky, but how can she *not* know who I am? Everyone knows *Razor's Edge*. Don't they?"

Her friend let out a deep breath. "Well, look at it this way. I love the song *'Moves Like Jagger'* and I know it's by *Maroon 5*. But I couldn't tell you any other songs they have, let alone the names or faces of the band members. She may not know any other songs by your group. Don't take it personally."

He nodded, and his eyes found Grace in the crowd again, now chatting with a small group of people.

"You know, it would be okay if you want to talk to her," Hope said.

"That's okay. I'm enjoying the view. Besides, she's doing her thing. I can tell she's good at working the crowd." It also gave him a chance to finally learn more about this intriguing woman. "What kind of guys does she like? What kind of guy has she dated?"

"I, um… I have no clue if Grace has dated anyone in the past three years."

"Really?" Blaze asked.

"I live too far away," she whispered.

BLAZE DIDN'T GET another encounter with Grace during the party. He really wanted to. She fascinated him. Not only did she not know who he was, prior to that evening, she didn't know about his past. His mistakes. She was his chance at a fresh start, a clean slate.

One of his favorite parts of the night was watching the way she interacted with everyone. He could understand why her costar had fallen for her.

Blaze loved that she had such a flirtatious personality, but she was oblivious to her bewitching of those around her. Every man she spoke with had a smile on his face when she walked away.

He had no doubt the theater company would have multiple new benefactors before the function ended.

Watching her fed his curiosity. If she was flirtatious by nature, what would she be like if she was truly interested in someone?

He was determined to find out.

CHAPTER 7

GRACE GLANCED OVER AT HOPE, STANDING WITH NICK AND BLAZE, and felt a twinge of jealousy. It only lasted a moment, but it was enough to make her heart speed up.

She needed to get away from Blaze, for more reasons than one. She hadn't meant to offend him but it was for the better. Even though the 'lady' in her scoffed at her lack of etiquette.

She would've rather spent the evening with Hope, since she rarely saw her friend, but she had work to do.

"Grace." Jason pulled her over to a short, stout gray-haired man. "I'd like you to meet Richard. He'll be signing on tomorrow as one of our new benefactors for the theater company."

"So pleased to meet you, sir." She took his outstretched hand. He had a tight grip. She gave him back the same, not afraid to put pressure in a handshake.

"Jason has been so kind to allow me to share some news with you, my dear." The man's voice was calming, like that of a loving grandfather. "It seems, you, dear Grace, are being offered a permanent acting position with the company."

"We've never done that for anyone before," Jason said.

She didn't know what to say, she was honored. *And* terrified.

"I purchased an old 1920s movie theater, and I'm renovating it into a live stage theater. I'm offering it as a permanent location for your company."

"I'm sorry?" Grace asked. The words going right over her head.

"Welcome to L.A., darling. I'm going to make you a star."

She blinked.

What?

She swallowed a few times as everything began to sink in.

"You'll need to relocate to Los Angeles, but that won't be a problem, will it? Since you haven't been home in almost four and a half months, it should be an easy break."

She *hated* paying for an apartment she wasn't living in. No doubt, all her plants had died. However, could she leave Colorado permanently? Her last memories of her parents were there. Was she ready to let go?

"Grace," Jason said, getting right in front of her, and in her personal bubble. "You can tell *no one* in the production. Not even Charles. Is that understood?"

She nodded.

"All right. We will meet up on Monday morning at Richard's theater to go over details. Congratulations. You've earned it. Now go, get out of costume and enjoy the rest of the night."

Her heart raced. All the new things that could come from this would improve her life.

"The party's winding down," Grace told Hope when she could return to her friend. "I've got to get out of costume. I'll be quick but it usually takes me about forty-five minutes. Do you want to meet back at the hotel or hang out here?"

"Actually," Nick said. "There's a bar right across the street. Blaze and I would be more than glad to keep Hope company."

Blaze wasn't with him.

Grace looked around the crowd, not seeing who she searched for. "I should apologize to Blaze. I was rude. But I'm not sure I have it in me to have another late night, though."

"Just come for a little while," Hope said. "I'll make sure you leave early enough."

She hugged her bestie before heading backstage to clean herself up.

She'd never gotten out of her costume so fast before. She washed her face, fixed her hair and redid her makeup. Blaze was bad news, in such a good way. She needed to stay away from him. Her heart couldn't take another destruction.

Why was he haunting her brain?

No! I can't look at him that way! I'm single for a reason. That can't change.

"Grace, do you mind if we have that talk real quick?" Charles appeared at her side with an almost-creepy precision, and Grace jumped.

His expression was full of sadness and her stomach jumped. She didn't have time to talk now; Hope and the guys were waiting for her, but maybe it was best they do this.

She nodded. "Okay."

Her costar took her hand and led her to the stage. They sat at the edge in the center, their feet dangling into the orchestra pit. Only the backstage lights illuminated the otherwise dark space. He took her hand into his own, again.

Grace looked down at their clasped hands, then he brought them up to kiss her knuckles.

"Are we all good then?" she asked.

"We've always been good. But my question is, where do we stand now?" His question dripped desperation.

"Charles, you're one of my dearest friends. I'm not looking for a relationship right now. I know you don't want to hear that, but I just don't feel that way about you." She made her voice steady and soft, but direct. Grace needed him to believe her. She was sincere and didn't want to hurt him, but 'they' could never be.

Not even if she'd never met Blaze.

Now is not the time to think about him!

"I don't buy it," he said. His mouth was screwed up in a defensive line.

"What don't you buy?" She tugged her hand free of his grip and tried to tamp her anger. She didn't want to yell. "Damn it, Charles, you're about to ruin everything. We have such a wonderful friendship, why do you want to ruin it?"

"You have feelings for me, Grace. Why won't you admit it? Kiss me. Like you did the day we met. Prove there's nothing there."

"Why can't you leave things the way it's always been? I just want my friend back." She pushed to her feet. She was done.

He latched onto her fingers, again, and tugged. "Please. Just one kiss. If there's nothing there, I'll let you go."

She sighed. He'd never drop this. She didn't want to kiss him.

Their friendship was already on the rocks.

"I'm sorry, but no. There is no point. It won't change things. Even if it did, I am in no place to start a relationship."

He stood and moved slowly toward her.

It felt like a cheesy movie.

Charles reached for her, his hand went to the nape of her neck and his fingers entwined in her hair.

Grace put her hands on his hard chest, pushing him back, but he didn't budge.

"Kiss me," he pleaded.

"I'm sorry, Charles. We don't have the chemistry you want. You need to let me go."

She meant those words, in more way than one.

He sighed, releasing his hold on her.

Grace took a step back. She was already late. Being the

graceful girl she was, her red heel caught on the hem of her jeans, causing her to stumble.

Charles caught her in his arms.

They both laughed.

"Just like the day we met, you've fallen into my arms," Charles said.

"You became my best friend after that," she reminded him.

"Always."

Her heart skipped. Was her friend back? Was she all forgiven?

They left the stage, and were headed for the exit when Jason called to Charles.

"Can I see you for a moment before you leave?"

GRACE HURRIED across the street to the small dive bar; she let her eyes adjust to the dark interior as she stepped inside. She looked straight back and saw the long bar, hundreds of liquor bottles lined up behind the bartender. Scattered all throughout were tables and chairs with various people standing around. To the right was a large dance floor and to the left was four pool tables. And Hope and the guys. Her dear friend was bent over with Nick behind her, showing her how to shoot properly.

Blaze was leaning up against the wall watching them. He must've felt her eyes on him; he looked her way. Even from the distance, his eyes lit up.

He pushed off the wall and closed the distance between them.

Blaze pulled her into his arms for an embrace, like they'd known each other for years.

Grace wasn't prepared for that. Instinct made her tug back. "Umm, hi Blaze?"

He chuckled when he released her and stepped back.

"Come to the bar with me, and get a drink?" Hope appeared beside them.

When they got to the bar, her friend leaned into the counter. Her smile said she had a secret. "You need to have a drink."

"Thank you, but I'll wait until tomorrow."

"No, Grace, you won't. You need to celebrate tonight."

"Not until tomorrow. I give certain things up during a production."

"You need to be honest with yourself. I know you forgo liquor for your plays, but you gave up having relationships *permanently*. You really need to move on."

Grace felt her back go ramrod stiff and her hands clenched tight. Her friends words were too much, She blew out the breath she held and started to walk away. Hope grabbed her arm, spinning her friend back to face her.

"I don't mean the loss of your parents, damn it! I meant *him*... You can't let one bad night with some asshole ruin the rest of your life! He wins if you never let yourself live! I think you have a very hot man just feet away, ready to bend over backwards for you. Or bend you over backwards. Either way, it's time."

Her friend was right. The timing was wrong. Hadn't she just told Charles she was in no place to start something?

Damn you, Charles. Even if I was ready to start a relationship with someone, you would hate me, because it's not with you.

"I overheard something tonight, on my way to the ladies room," Hope said, changing the subject. "About you permanently joining the company?"

Grace could only stare at Hope.

"So it's true? That's amazing and definitely something to celebrate! It's only one drink."

Hope was right.

She could use a drink. It'd been a really long day.

Her bestie pulled her cellphone out of her back pocket and looked at the screen. Then she laughed.

"What's so funny?"

"I have this awesome app called *Mixology*. It tells you how to make different kinds of drinks. We have to have *this* one." Hope flashed the picture on the screen.

Grace laughed with her and agreed.

With their drinks in hand, they headed back to the pool table, and Nick and Blaze.

The men grinned.

Blaze cocked his head to the side when he saw her drink. "Hope said you weren't drinking until Sunday. Did something change?"

"Yeah. We both agreed I needed to celebrate tonight."

"So, what're you drinking?"

"Hope said it's called *Nick at Night*. It's an ass kicker. I know for sure it has tequila."

"*Nick at Night*? What about *BJ in the morning*?" he teased.

Grace arched an eyebrow.

He chuckled. Then he pointed at Nick. "Nick… at night." Then he pointed to himself. "BJ…in the morning."

"So, It's BJ instead of Blaze? What would a BJ in the morning entail?"

He laughed again, long and hard. "An ounce of music, an ounce dancing, and fill the rest with seduction."

"Well, that sounds delicious. I guess I'd better go to the bartender and see if he can hook me up." Grace giggled, playing along. After her confrontation with Charles, she could use a little fun.

"Ouch." He grabbed his chest. "That hurt."

She winked and dared him to continue their banter.

GRACE SET her empty glass on the table. She and Blaze watched Hope and Nick finished their game of pool.

When his friend racked the balls to prepare for another game, Blaze disappeared to the bar.

"Hey, Gracie," Nick said. "You're up next."

"Umm, okay. So, who am I playing?"

"Well, I beat Hope, so I guess you're playing me."

Hope flashed a devilish grin.

"I'm warning you, Nick. I suck," Grace admitted. The tequila from her first drink in months was already kicking in.

Blaze came back to the pool table with a bright blue drink in his hand and offered it to her.

"What's this?" she asked.

"It's a *BJ in the Morning*." He winked.

Grace hesitantly took the glass and brought it to her lips. It was so sweet and she couldn't taste the alcohol. This would be problematic.

She needed to handle this one very slowly. The drink, too. She thanked him and set it on the little table.

"Grace, you have to break to determine if you're solids or stripes," Nick said.

The liquor had more than kicked in, and she was feeling extremely flirtatious. She purposely messed up when scattering the balls. She wanted the guys to think she didn't know how to play pool very well.

"I can help you, if you'd like," Blaze offered.

She found herself in the same position Hope had been in with Nick just a short time before. She was so glad she had her skinny jeans and red heels on.

He had his chest to her back as they both leaned over the pool table. "Just look straight down the stick. Pretend it is a line, showing you where to go."

Little did they know Grace was an expert. Her father had taught her from a young age how to play. It was fun to keep playing games with Blaze.

She winked at Hope. Her friend knew the truth about her experience. On more than one occasion, they'd come home from the bar with more money than they'd started with because men would bet they could beat Grace.

After a few more turns with help from Blaze, she told him she'd finally gotten the hang of how to play. When it wasn't her turn, she kept going back to the little table to sip her blue drink. Although she was now extremely intoxicated, Grace kicked Nick's ass at pool.

"Hey," he exclaimed. "I thought you said you suck."

She laughed, the alcohol speaking for her. She glanced at Blaze. "I do suck. I suck good."

His face flushed crimson.

Hope burst out laughing.

There were a couple guys waiting for them to finish their round so they could have a turn, so Nick suggested they hit the dance floor.

GRACE HADN'T HAD alcohol in over four months, so the two drinks she had hit her hard. She moved seductively on the dance floor, letting the music drive her body.

She didn't blink an eye when Blaze came up behind her, slipping his hands on her hips. She'd never felt so sexy before, and they fit so perfectly together.

His hands splayed across her abdomen and she felt a tightening within her. He was touching her like he had in her dream.

Just like in that delicious dream, Grace had to see his eyes.

She turned in his arms and they continued to move in a perfect fluid dance. Their eyes locked, the intensity burning between them. She didn't want to close her eyes, afraid he'd disappear.

His soft lips touched hers and she was lost in the kiss.

He gently probed her mouth and their tongues began the seductive dance their bodies had started.

Grace had been kissed before, but it had never been like this.

Fire started at the base her neck and filled her entire form, all the way down to her toes.

In that one moment, they were alone.

She didn't remember leaving the bar or entering the hotel, but everything after the door closed, would be forever etched in her mind.

CHAPTER 8

CHARLES FOLLOWED JASON. WHAT COULD THE MAN POSSIBLY NEED?

They walked in silence to the office just past the entrance to the dressing rooms, the only sound was the clop-clop of their shoes. He couldn't take his mind off what happened with Grace and what she had said.

"Damn it, Charles, you're about to ruin everything."

No. He was trying to make things better.

He'd been waiting five months for this moment. Why couldn't she see that?

His shoulders tightened and he became agitated, hearing her words in his head again.

"I'm sorry, Charles. We don't have the chemistry you want."

They had chemistry.

That was what made the play a huge success; the way they were meant for each other. Like their characters. Maddie and Louis started out as secret friends, then she was kidnapped and seduced by Der Hahn. It took that tragic affair for her to realize Louis *was* her true love.

"Come on in." Jason pulled him back to the moment. He opened the door to the office, flicking on a harsh overhead light.

Charles blinked a few times, his eyes not quite adjusted to the change.

"Have a seat. We need to chat."

He cringed. No one liked hearing those four words together. It never boded well for the recipient. He sat in a chair that matched the desk.

"I want to thank you for pushing me at auditions to choose Grace for Maddie. You had a good eye and I'm grateful for that. She has been an asset to the company I never knew I needed." His boss sat on the edge of the mahogany desk crossing his ankles, looking down on Charles.

"I told you, I needed her." He stumbled. "You needed her. She *is* Maddie."

"Indeed. With the show ending, though, I feel it is my responsibility to pull you aside and point something out. I see the way you look at her. When you're not in character. I'm a little concerned."

"Excuse me?" This was none of Jason's business.

"I've seen it before. You have feelings for your costar. Don't deny it. We've *all* seen it." The man he worked for stood and began pacing the room.

"And…" Charles began, knowing his 'boss' wasn't done yet.

"*And* I think you need to take a step back. Look at the big picture here. We only have one more show, and after tomorrow night, you many never see her again. You need to let go."

"*You need to let me go.*"

He heard Grace's words coming from Jason.

"I know you're wrong. She *does* have feelings for me." He rushed to his feet. The chair scraped across the concrete floor. "She's just waiting for the show to end. That's how professional she is. You'll see." He didn't wait to see if Jason had anymore unwanted options. He spun on his heels and stormed out of the office.

He returned to the darkness of center stage, where Grace's scent still lingered.

Fuck you, Jason! You wouldn't know love if it ran your sorry tanned ass over!

Had the man not been watching their performance that night? It'd been so emotional. Charles had felt the turmoil his character went through, seeing the girl he loved being pulled away from him.

At the wine party, he'd been watching her flit from group to group, laughing and smiling as they chatted her up. He noticed the way she interacted with all the other men in the room. It wasn't so much that she was flirting; she just had such an effervescent personality, all people were drawn to her.

She may not have meant for him to fall in love with her, but it was done nonetheless.

He wasn't giving up. She *would* be his.

She said she loves me.

His hand lovingly caressed the hardwood of the stage where Grace had previously been sitting.

He needed her to kiss him; kiss him and *mean* it.

She said no.

Charles wanted so badly to *make* her do it.

It'd taken all his restraint to let her walk away.

One more night. I can wait one more night.

Across the street from the theater, he saw the neon sign for a bar. A stiff drink was exactly what he needed. The single glass of wine he'd had at just an hour ago had done nothing for him. He needed a little help if he was going to make it through the night.

When he pushed open the door to the bar, he could swear Grace's scent was still around him. He breathed it in and held it for a moment, slowly letting it out as he went to get to get a drink. "Double Jack and Coke, light on the ice." Charles turned away after ordering, leaning his back against the edge, and he took in the view around him.

The club scene wasn't his thing; he always seemed to get recognized. However, this place was the type of bar that none of his fans would be found dead in. It was more like a biker bar than a dance club.

Perfect.

He watched a couple moving seductively on the dance floor, wishing it was Grace with him, seducing each other through music and movement. His cock twitched. If only Grace pressed herself against him like that woman was doing to some lucky chap.

The bartender grabbed his attention, his drink was ready.

Charles started a tab and returned to his people watching. He took a slow sip of his cold libation, then almost dropped the glass when he glanced to the right side of the room. There, bent over a pool table with Blaze far too close, was *his* Grace.

He set the glass down with the clank, causing some of the contents to spill over the rim. This was the last thing he'd expected to see. Hadn't she had gone back to the hotel with the rest of the cast?

She didn't drink, so what the fuck was she doing there?

With Blaze?

Friend of not, he wanted to kill the man.

His brother's words from the night before came crashing back. *"I think you still have competition, little brother."*

Blaze? That was his competition?

I don't think so, old friend.

This was just another scene that needed to play out.

In the show when Maddie was kidnapped, Louis had to fight off the roustabouts. However, there was no one here for him to fight, besides Blaze.

Charles picked up his drink and downed it in just a few gulps, not once coming up for a breath of air. He waved to the bartender. "Another."

He tried to take his eyes off of Grace with Blaze; anything to calm the rage building inside him. The cold of his drink helped soothe the burning in his cheeks, but the liquor only fueled the fire in his belly.

He wanted to rush across the room, rip his old friend from her side, and pummel his face until he was no longer recognizable. What little sanity he was gripping tightly to, reminded him it would make matters worse.

Charles had to wait.

He scanned the room again. In the far corner, past the dance floor, and thankfully as far away from the pool table as could be, there was a punching bag hanging from the ceiling next to a pinball machine.

Exactly what he needed.

If he couldn't beat the shit out of Blaze, then he could take it out on the punching bag.

He slid the bartender at five dollar bill.

"Got change?"

"Dude, there's a coin machine right over there," the surly man pointed out.

Charles took back his money, grabbed his drink, and headed for the corner.

His knuckles burned, threatening to split open with the force he was dishing out to the bag. Throw after throw, he took all his anger and frustration out on the bag.

He only stopped long enough to pick up his drink and once again upend it.

Charles set the glass back down and saw out of the corner of his eye, her chestnut hair, the golden highlights illuminated by the lights on the small square dance floor.

She was alone, dancing to the beat of the music, her body moving lithely, seductively. Grace's eyes were closed, head tilted to one side, as she slowly turned in place.

He'd never seen anything so beautiful. His body reacted to the sight, his jeans far too tight for his growing erection. He touched it gingerly, wishing it was *her* hand on him.

Charles ran his palm up and down the length, feeling his cock pulsate as he watched her. His heart beat heavy with every boom of the bass. He took an involuntary step forward, wanting to touch her. To have her touch him.

Blaze stepped up behind her, putting his hands all over Grace, touching her in ways only *he* should touch her. Like a bucket of ice water over the head, his body went cold. His hands balled into tight fists, his knuckles protesting with pain.

Get a grip Charles, you have to wait. This is your Der Hahn. He's trying to seduce Maddie. He can't have her. In the end, she will *be mine.*

He bit the inside of his cheek, trying to bring an ounce of discomfort to ease the aching in his groin. It didn't help.

Charles sat at the little table, continuing to watch from the dark corner as Blaze ran his hands along Grace's stomach, like *he* did when they danced on stage.

The dark haired man turned her in his arms, wrapping them around her, his hands crossed at her waist.

When his old friend leaned in to capture Grace's lips, he shot up out of the seat, knocking the table over. The glass shattering as the empty drink hit the ground. He looked down at what he'd done, then around him to see if anyone had reacted.

No one looked his way.

He righted the table. After getting the chair back on all fours too, he looked back toward the dance floor. Grace and Blaze were gone.

Son of a bitch! He's taken her!

CHAPTER 9

Grace's heart thundered.

Blaze closed the hotel room door behind them.

The alcohol she'd consumed was doing nothing for the knots in her stomach. She'd never been the type of girl to be in a position like this.

Hope was right; I need to learn to live again.

She'd probably never see Blaze again after this weekend. So why not go for it?

Grace had been attracted to him from the moment they'd met, so making this choice was logical, right?

Blaze stepped back to her, tugging playfully at the hem of her red shirt, and bringing her fully into the room. With their eyes locked, he began undressing her. One by one he released each button, his knuckles grazing up her skin as they went.

Goosebumps danced along her skin.

His fingertips slipped across her collarbone until he could grasp her shirt in his hands, sliding it off her arms to let it flutter to the floor. She let out a sigh when he reached around and unhooked her bra. It joined her shirt.

Grace bit back a gasp when Blaze tenderly took her breasts into his hands.

His thumbs gently caressed, tightening her nipples to hard nubs. He dropped his head to take the right one into the heat of his mouth.

Her breath caught in her throat and she slipped her fingers into his dark hair, holding on as he tasted her flesh.

Blaze lifted his head only long enough to switch to the other breast. When he released her, she was panting.

I can't breathe and we are just getting started.

He reached for the waistband of her jeans, undoing the button and zipper. He knelt on the carpet and slowly peeled them down her body.

As he went, inch by slow delicious inch, he left a kiss on her hot skin. First on the hipbone, then her upper thigh.

Grace had to put her hands on his shoulders, so she wouldn't lose her balance when she stepped out of her pants.

First he removed her red heels so the denim could come off.

She finally got to feel like Cinderella as he took one shoe, then the other before helping remove her jeans, then her panties. She waited for Blaze to stand, but he didn't.

He sat back on his heels, looking up at her.

Her heart hammered in her ears. She was bare before this man she'd just met, offering him something she swore she would never again give. She was scared, but exhilarated, the alcohol giving her courage she otherwise wouldn't have.

Or stupidity, honey.

Grace leaned forward slightly to push back a lock of his hair that'd fallen forward.

He captured her hand. He turned her hand over and lightly traced her palm, followed by a soft kiss in the center.

Something so simple, and it had her letting out a breath she didn't know she'd been holding.

Blaze let her hand go and surprised her by running his fingers up the back of her legs. They almost gave out when he skimmed the crook of her knees, a very sensitive spot. He brought the light touch to her inner thighs and her body shook with anticipation.

She looked down, their eyes locking but still not a word said.

It was so intense.

His eyes seemed to change.

Darker.

Desire like she'd never seen.

Still on his knees, Blaze kissed both her hip bones, before he finally stood. He walked her backwards, until she met the bed. "Lay back," he whispered, kneeling down again.

Grace obeyed, glad to have the chance to break their locked gaze.

He slipped a hand beneath each leg to place them over his shoulders, giving him full access to her center. He tugged her to the edge of the bed.

She felt the heat of his mouth take over her most sensitive spot. She gripped the blankets on his bed as his tongue moved with precision, bringing her body to life.

Blaze knew what he was doing.

I can't believe I am doing this?!

He brought his hand up to hold her small patch of curls out of his way, so he could concentrate on her clit.

Far too quickly, as no man had done before, Grace's body responded and a climax built. His hand left her curls, to go who knew where.

Wrapped in the moment of the intense pressure within her, panic warred with what her brain told her was going on.

What's happening? Oh... My... God...

Blaze shifted slightly, but didn't stop his blissful torture on her body. He flicked his tongue with strength and speed, and her body tightened even more.

There was an explosion in her nether regions. Pleasure washed over her, chills throughout, but her skin was hot. The pulsing between her legs shot through the rest of her form, leaving her lightheaded.

An orgasm; she'd never had one before…

In the same moment, Blaze slipped her legs off his shoulders and rose.

He pressed against her sex and her body spasmed.

He entered her, just a little, as her body still convulsed, then pulled back and drove forward gently again.

"Blaze," she could barely whisper. She was still riding her very first orgasm.

His hands slid up her thighs to grip her hips as he pressed into her, all the way to the hilt. Blaze moved with a precision that told her he'd done this often and with great skill.

It should've bothered her, but the passion and the intoxication, made Grace not care.

He groaned and continued to move in and out, his fingers keeping possession of her, holding her tight.

She wanted to see his face as he took her. She needed to remember it on the nights she felt alone; a reminder of what she didn't intend to keep. "Blaze. Please," Grace pleaded.

He stopped his delicious thrusting, giving her a chance to prop herself up on her elbows and look at him.

Blaze was fully dressed.

Of course he is.

She reached out a hand and he helped her up, his erection slipping about of her. She stood up, standing right in front of him. "It's my turn," she said seductively. She unbuttoned his black shirt with the speed of an actor, use to little time for costume changes.

Grace slipped it off, chased by his white undershirt. She'd seen the tattoos on his neck and hands but was amazed by the amount he had hidden by his clothing. She touched the beautiful artwork on his left pec, tracing the outline of the design. Her fingers skimmed up his shoulders to trail down his arms, both were covered with colorful tattoos.

They're beautiful.

She looked up into his dark brown eyes as she grabbed for the waistband of his black jeans, slipping her hands over his hot skin.

Blaze trailed his fingertips along her bare arms, down to her hands, which were shaking with anticipation as she undressed him. "Do you trust me?" he whispered.

She'd trusted no one, with any capacity of herself, in so long, it was a foreign feeling. Grace trusted him, even if she wasn't sure why.

"Yes."

He took her hand and led her back to the bed, signaling for her to move to the center.

She rearranged the pillows for comfort and lay back, just enough lift from the pillows to not be completely flat on her back.

The mattress shifted as Blaze joined her on the bed, placing himself between her legs. He rested on his elbows, staring at her with such heat in his eyes; her ovaries might burst from the hormonal overdrive.

He pressed gently at her sex, and her body came back to life.

Her hips moved on their own, inviting him in deeper, wrapping her legs around his waist to give him all of her. Grace slid her hands over his fine backside, where she felt his muscles flex with each thrust. Her breathing came in hard raspy gasps as he took her to new places.

She had to bite her lower lip to keep from crying out; the intense building was happening inside her again.

This time it was different.

Grace couldn't think straight. Lightening burst behind her eyes and her muscles tightened around him. She *felt* the fullness of him in that moment.

Blaze continued to move, deeper, harder, riding the pulsations in her wall until he too, made a feral noise before shuddering, slowing, and ultimately collapsing forward to bury his face in her hair.

Damn... what have I been missing?

♪♫

WHEN SHE AWOKE, all her muscles hurt and her pillow was warm and hard. She moved her fingers ever so slightly. They were on warm flesh.

Her eyes snapped open and everything from the night before came flooding back. She tried to slide off the bed so she wouldn't wake him.

What have I done?

It took her a moment to find all of her clothing, they were scattered all over the room. She got dressed quickly and was about to open the door when she heard him call her.

"Grace? Where're you going?" Blaze's voice was just as tired-sounding as she felt.

She released the handle.

He was so beautiful. What she needed to say tore her heart.

"I have to get back to the theater. We have another performance tonight, remember?"

"The show's not until this evening. Come back to bed." He patted the mattress.

"Blaze…"

How could she tell him the truth without hurting his feelings?

This couldn't be anything other than a one-night stand.

I promised myself to never love again.

She let out a deep sigh. "I've… I've got to go."

"Is everything all right?"

She could hear the hurt in his voice.

"Yeah, it's just…" Grace leaned against the wall. Words deserted her.

"I'll see you tonight?"

His voice was so hopeful.

Was he expecting more?

She couldn't offer more.

She was in no position to start a relationship with anyone.

Hadn't she tried explaining this to Charles the night before?

How did she end up in this situation?

Grace just nodded, and left, letting the door slam behind her.

CHAPTER 10

GRACE SAT AT HER DRESSING TABLE STARING AT THE WOMAN IN THE reflection.

Who are you? This certainly isn't me. Is it?

The woman in the mirror looked like she had gotten no sleep the night before, yet, her eyes were bright.

Her lips were red and full, still bruised from a night of passion. Her head full of chestnut hair was a tangled mess, and her cheeks were rosy.

She looked so beautiful.

Why do I feel so horrible inside? I just spend the most magical night of my life in the arms of the most amazing man and I walked away.

She wiped at tears she couldn't stop from falling.

I shouldn't have had that drink. I should've stayed away. No matter how charming and handsome he is, I won't become like my mom... I don't want Blaze in my life. I don't need him, or any man, ever!

Her parents had had a love only found in movies and romance novels. True love. Once upon a time, she'd wanted that, too.

Until she met Zack.

He'd been kind and romantic, just like her father. Then he'd torn her heart into a million pieces. She'd assumed her virginity would be the doorway opening the relationship she'd thought they had.

Instead, he'd laughed, *thanked* her, and walked away.

Grace had sworn she'd never love another man.

She hadn't.

For years.

Her heart couldn't get broken again, if she kept it to herself.

"But I'm doing to Blaze, what Zack did. 'Thanks for last night, but I gotta move on.'" She wouldn't allow the guilt to overtake her. She just couldn't go there with Blaze. She'd just landed her dream job. "The theater's my life now. I don't need or want anyone else in it. Not Charles, not Blaze. Just me. I only need me."

She took a deep breath but that was a mistake. Blaze's scent was all over her. Her chest tightened.

She gingerly touched her lips, remembering the way they'd felt against with his. Her cheeks flush hot when she remembered all the delicious things he'd done to her body.

Grace had never known she could feel such things, that her body could do the things they had.

Blaze had been so sweet and caring.

He'd seen to her needs before his own.

She'd never felt so special. Grace could've spent the rest of her life wrapped in his arms. That wasn't in the plans. She had one last show to do; then her life was going to completely change.

The next few hours were a blur as she hung out in the dressing rooms, not wanting to head back to her hotel.

She could've stood in the showers in the ladies room until the water ran cold. Instead, the tips of her fingers wrinkled and it was time to get out.

Grace went in search of Pete, their head makeup artist.

"So nice of you to 'Grace' us with your presence." He laughed at his own pun. "You look hungover, or exhausted, or freshly fucked. And since we all know you don't drink, and you're in bed every night by midnight, that would leave us with..." He cocked his head to the side, like he was thinking about something. "Charles came in today in a foul mood, so you definitely weren't freshly..."

She scoffed before he could finish what he was going to say. "What makes you think I have any interest in Charles?"

"Whether or not you have an interest in him, the whole company knows he has interest in you. So maybe you did get some last night. And that's why he's in a foul mood because it wasn't him."

Grace's cheeks flush with heat.

How did Charles know what happened last night? And did anyone else in the company know?

She shook herself for being paranoid. Charles was probably just upset their talk didn't go well. She half-dreaded their last show because of it. She'd have to look him in the eye.

"Haha," Pete said and he clasped his hands together. "You did get some! Tonight's show will *definitely* be interesting. Have a seat in my chair, darling and let me make you beautiful."

GRACE HAD BEEN RIGHT ABOUT NOT WANTING to deal with Charles. Veiled anger was in his eyes, pointed in her direction the entire show.

When Louis got angry with Maddie and decided to go out and seek his fortune and women, Grace could hear the anger bled into Charles's voice more than what was necessary for his character.

Everything about his performance was aggressive.

Just like the night before, they only had a short time to talk between sets. It felt like *déjà vu* as she pulled him aside.

"Charles, what the hell's going on? This is our last show and you're screwing things up!"

Rage burned in his eyes. "I'm not the one that's screwing

anything, *you* are. I thought you didn't want to start a relationship?" he spat.

"I'm not. We already discussed this. What is this really about?"

"I watched you last night, with *BJ*. I should've known. My brother and his friends, they always get the girls."

"You mean Blaze? Is this about me dancing with him at the bar last night?" Grace was too angry to blush, but...he'd watched her?

"Don't play stupid. We both know you did more than just dance with him. I saw you leave in a hurry."

Grace gasped. Was he really going down that road? She put her hands on her hips and glared. "Blaze and I are my business. *Not* yours. It had nothing to do with you."

"If you were going to be with anyone, it should've been me. I asked you to kiss me, ME! The man you claim you love—"

She interrupted him. "You're twisting my words! I'm not having this conversation again. I'll see you on stage." She fled to her side of the theater.

The magic they'd had the previous night in the ending scene wasn't there this time.

Charles was still angry and there was nothing Grace could do about the way he felt. She'd already told him there'd never be a chance between them; she just didn't feel that way about him.

He was just going to have to get a clue.

The show ended, and the applause was overwhelming. She was sad it was over.

Tomorrow would start her new future and she was excited to see where it went.

This was supposed to be her party night; the night she could get totally and completely drunk and not care about it. Now Grace was worried about the consequences from the night before.

To celebrate the end of the show, Jason was throwing a party in the ballroom where the masquerade had happened just forty-eight hours before.

She didn't want to go.

Grace was first to the dressing room. When she got to her table, Pete standing there.

He had his huge makeup case sitting on her countertop next to her bag of Reese's Pieces, which were scattered on the counter.

"My darling, Grace. I need to make you look fabulous!"

"Um, okay... Why?" She had no need to impress. Last night was the wooing show, with the cheese and wine party. Tonight was just cast and friends. She could go in her pajamas if she wanted.

"I was at the masquerade *and* the cheese and wine party, darling. I may be gay, but I can still see when a man has his eye out for a woman."

Grace snorted. That seemed to be her sound of choice lately. "I already told you, I have no interest in Charles. He's just my friend."

"I wasn't talking about him. I was talking about that tattooed hottie. I couldn't keep my eyes off him, and he couldn't keep his eyes off you. I didn't think about it until after you were on stage, but that's your hook up, right?"

Heat suffused her neck and face. She was probably fifty shades of red.

That was all the answer Pete needed.

"If you let go of that fine piece of—"

Grace slashed her hand through the air, but she sat in the make-up chair. "Pete! Last night shouldn't have happened. I don't have time for a relationship. My life is about to get really complicated. I can't ..." Tears filled her eyes.

Blaze was such an amazing man, and any woman would be lucky to get to know him better, but she had to keep moving forward. She'd worked so hard and given up so much to be where she was headed.

She grabbed a handful of Reese's; they always made her feel better. She shoved a few in her mouth to keep her from having to continue.

"Well, sweetie. If you don't want him all the time, at least enjoy him a little before you let him go."

"No!" she cried, almost choking on the candy pieces in her mouth. "I could never do that!"

"Come on Grace, live a little." Pete turned his back to her to get his make-up case open. He came back with a makeup brush in one hand and a compact in the other.

Grace swallowed the remaining candy and wiped at the tears that fell.

He sighed when he saw them. "Someone did that to you?"

She sobbed. She never cried, and now she was an emotional mess.

Pete brought her into a tight hug. "Sorry, sweetie. I feel your pain ... Let me go get something to soothe your skin, crying does havoc on your face." He didn't wait for her to answer; just walked away.

Grace sat alone for only a moment before the rest of the girls filed into the room. She picked up her make-up remover wipe and scrubbed at her face again, hoping no one could tell she'd been crying.

They did their own things, not paying much attention to her other than a few 'good jobs' and 'can you believe it's over's'.

She was grateful for that.

Pete returned with wonderful soothing spray that reminded her of cucumbers. He spritzed her face and had her sit still for a moment.

She breathed deep and tried to relax.

Soon, her makeup guy was doing his magic and made her look ready to hit the town, or in this case, the ballroom.

Grace slipped on her green, spaghetti strapped gown, took

Pete's hand, and they walked to the hotel together, just a block away.

CHAPTER 11

Blaze had never been in a situation like this. *He* was usually the one that left the room, never to look back.

This time, somehow this woman had worked her way into his heart. From the moment he'd seen her in the ballroom, he'd been mesmerized.

The magnificence of her gown and mask were lost to the beauty of her personality. The mask hid her face, but it was her smile that'd drawn his attention, followed by her laugh.

When he had been introduced to her, it was her blue-green eyes that'd called to him. He'd just had to know more—everything—about this woman.

When she'd found out he was a star, she hadn't cared. It wasn't something he was used to. Usually, his career had the women falling at his feet—even when he didn't want them to.

Not Grace.

I've never felt drawn to anyone like this before.

Blaze sat a table with Nick and Hope, the ice melting in the untouched drink he held.

He'd dated many beautiful women and in the beginning, it'd

been nice to be loved for his talent. But he was more than just a member of *Razor's Edge*.

Those relationships were never quite right.

He finally picked up his drink and took a large gulp.

I shouldn't have taken advantage of her drunken stage. I know better. But last night, playing pool, she fit so perfectly. It wasn't just sexual. When she kissed me, it just seemed right.

He couldn't get his mind off Grace. She must've been thinking about him as well, because her performance wasn't like it had been the night before.

She walked through the doors to the afterparty, wrapped around the arm of a tall slender man. Grace was radiant in the green gown.

Blaze recalled those long legs wrapped tightly around him the night before, and how he wanted them there again.

She took two steps down into the ballroom, but tripped on the third and final step. She must've caught her heel on the back of her gown.

He wanted to jump right up and run to her, but before he was out of his seat, she was already righted and laughing about it. Blaze heard Hope giggle, and his gaze broke away from her.

"Dude, hello?" Nick said.

"Yeah, I know what you mean," Blaze said, hoping the generic answer would appease him; he just wanted to go to Grace.

"You know what I mean about what? I asked you if you wanted to join Hope and me tomorrow to check out some sights in L.A.."

Blaze flushed; it was a weird feeling because he never blushed.

Just then, as if to save him, Grace came to his side.

Hope left her high bar chair to hug her friend. She whispered something in Grace's ear, but he didn't catch it.

Whatever it was made Grace's cheeks pink and her eyes sparkle, so Blaze was a fan.

She smiled in his direction. It was timid, like she was scared or nervous. "Hello, Blaze." Her voice was almost a whisper.

"Grace." Blaze jumped off his bar stool and extended his hand to her.

She hesitantly offered her own back.

He tenderly kissed her knuckles, wishing they were alone and he could continue upwards. "Your performance tonight was beautiful."

Her cheeks flushed pink again and he liked that as much as she loved the spotlight, she was still humble.

"As sad as I am it's over, I'm also grateful. My life is about to make some major changes." She still spoke so quietly, nothing like her normal outgoing flirtatious ways.

He took this as a good sign. Hadn't he just been thinking the night before what she would be like if she really had feelings for someone? Blaze gestured to the empty bar stool beside him. "Wanna join us?"

She nodded her hands falling to rest in her lap when she sat.

Blaze was very curious to know why she seemed so timid. "Can I order you a drink?"

Her expression said she was seriously debating the question. When she finally replied, it stung him.

"Yes, please. Anything but a *'BJ in the Morning'* though."

He must've failed to hide his hurt.

Grace reached for his hand, which had been resting on the bar beside her. "I didn't mean it that way!" she cried, her eyes turning red. "I just don't want to get so drunk again, and it was really powerful."

Blaze tried to shake off his reaction. She seemed sincere, and he didn't want to call her a liar. He ordered her a glass of Moscato. When he studied her expression, real concern shot up from his gut.

This was about more than just sex. Personally, he'd never had a connection like they'd shared. He didn't understand it. Maybe she was struggling, too?

He took a deep breath and spoke with a heavy heart. "Grace, I can tell something's going on. Are you upset with me about last night?" Blaze didn't give her a chance to answer; just plowed on. "I know you were a little drunk, and I shouldn't have taken advantage of that. I should say I am sorry, but I'm not." He had so much more to say, but her tears fell. Indecision made him fidget. He grabbed a napkin, handing it to her.

Grace took the napkin and dabbed at her eyes. She took a deep breath and tried to speak.

Whatever she was about to say didn't come out the first time she tried. Her mouth hung open, then she swallowed. A few more seconds passed before she could get it out.

"Last night was the best night of my life, in so many ways, but—"

"Why did you leave this morning?"

"I had to get back to the theater," she said.

She was lying.

"That's bullshit, Grace. Just tell me the truth." Blaze hadn't meant to be so rough, he just wanted the truth.

"I'm so sorry." More tears fell, then she jumped up from her barstool and ran away. Grace rushed to the ladies room.

"What was that about?" Nick leaned in closer.

"I'm not entirely sure. But I'm determined to find out." Blaze headed toward the ladies room. He was going to get her to talk to him, one way or the other.

GRACE COULDN'T STOP CRYING. She ran to the bathroom, hoping for a small escape.

She wanted nothing more than to kiss his beautiful lips again and relive last night.

I can't! I already felt like I used him once; I won't do it again.

She wiped at her eyes and took a few calming breaths. She wasn't like *this*. She never cried, yet he was making her an emotional wreck.

I'm turning into my mother! We've just met and I can already feel the ache in my body thinking of never seeing him again! I have to tell him why I can't do this.

She stood a little taller and took a deep breath before stepping out of the door.

Grace wasn't expecting to see Blaze standing right there.

He said nothing; just offered his hand.

She looked at it, then up to his eyes.

They were such a rich chocolate color, but it was the turmoil in them that caught her breath. She clasped his fingers. Worries about what would happen flipped her tummy. Was she willing to find out?

Blaze walked her across the ballroom and out through the double glass doors that opened to the patio-area.

The ballroom was on the tenth floor so the balcony looked out over the city. Eight or so small potted trees scattered along the walls of the balcony were lit with strings of twinkle lights, illuminating the area. It was the only light out there, but it was enough.

It seemed like the sky was threatening to open up and rain.

The theater was a few buildings away, and just across from that, was the little dive bar that'd started it all—other than the masquerade ball, of course. Grace sighed and turned to face him. "Blaze, I'm sorry. You have every right to know why I left you this morning. Please don't take it personally; it's—"

"Don't say *that*." He put his fingers on her lips to silence her.

She grabbed his hand and kissed his fingertips before she pushed them away. "It *is* me. I can't give you the relationship you deserve. To be honest, I'm not ready for that."

"Why not?"

She wasn't ready to give him the truth, to say the words out loud. So she lied.

"My life's too hectic right now."

"I, more than anyone, know what it's like to have a girlfriend and a crazy hectic life. I've done it before."

"And how did that turn out?" she asked.

"Not so well, but it wasn't because of the life, it was the girl. She didn't understand what my life was like."

"And you think I would?" As much as she wished she could be with him, she was absolutely terrified. After Zack had ruined her, she never wanted to try having a relationship again.

"This isn't really about your crazy life, is it?" he asked.

"It is. Tomorrow I'm meeting at an old theater to find out where my life will be. I was offered a permanent position with the theater company and I don't know what that means. I'll have to move here, to L.A., but other than that..." she trailed off.

"Grace, I live in L.A.. And, I'm familiar with being in the limelight and balancing real life. I'd be here for you, someone to help you adjust to everything. Don't let that be what holds us back. But that's not it, I can see it in your eyes; hear it in your voice. What is this *really* about?"

Grace slid away, not to leave, but to breathe, and to put her thoughts into words.

A fantastic bolt of lightning lit up the sky, the thunder rumbling right behind it.

"Why would someone like you want me?" she whispered as she turned to face him.

"Are you serious?" Blaze took a step closer. "What's that supposed to mean, *someone like me?*" He took another step closer.

"You've dated beautiful women; it sounds like you could have anyone. So why *me?*"

"You can ask me that? After last night? How could you doubt I want you?" Blaze cupped her cheek. The warmth of his skin filled her with heat.

She was trying so hard not to cry, which was stupid. Sex aside, she didn't know Blaze. They'd met forty-eight hours ago, right? Why did it feel like more? Like she'd known him for years.

"Beauty isn't just in looks. It's in how you treat others; it's who you are on the inside. Just watching you make everyone smile, it melted me. I've had so many failed relationships and yesterday, at the party, I knew I'd never have that with you. You care about everyone. You made sure they all had smiles before you left them. I watched as those smiles stayed, even after you had moved on. Do you have any idea what you do to people, to me?"

How could she have this incredibly sexy man in front of her tell her she was that special? Her heart thundered as much as the sky.

"Tell me about the man that hurt you so bad?" he whispered when she didn't speak.

Her eyes snapped up to lock with his.

"How did you know? I mean, that I was hurt?"

His cheeks flushed red and surprise washed over her.

"I'm ashamed to say, I've been that man. I've hurt women. Love them and leave them and all. The life of a pop star. I can't make excuses for what I've done, but I've learned. So, who was he?"

Grace was afraid he'd laugh at her inexperience, but knew telling the truth would be the only way he'd understand. Even if it wasn't the whole truth. "Zack was my best friend right after high school. He was funny, exciting, and he cared about me. Or so I thought. I was sure he was my true love and we'd live happily ever after. Turned out, I was just a bet. Just one more girl to deflower. It broke me. My parents had set the bar pretty high for what love should be. After my first and last sexual experience, I swore off men. Completely."

Blaze startled. "Wait. Last night... it was your second time. Like, Ever?"

Heat kissed the back of her neck and cheeks. She nodded because she couldn't find the words. Again.

His Adam's apple bobbed as he swallowed. Twice. "Come. Here. Now." He pulled her up against him, holding her close.

She rested her cheek on his shoulder and he kissed her bare skin. "You should know I'm not like him. I'd never hurt you like that. Please, give us a chance."

He moved just slightly so she'd look up at him.

Her heart slid into overdrive as Grace pondered what he was about to offer.

Can I do this?

She closed her eyes, prepared for his lips to touch hers.

She heard, as much as felt, Blaze get ripped from her arms.

Grace opened her eyes to see Charles throw a punch to her lover's left cheek.

CHAPTER 12

BLAZE BARELY HAD A MOMENT TO SEE WHO'D HIT HIM BEFORE HE was tackled at the waist and knocked to the ground by Charles.

The *boy* he'd known for almost twelve years looked at him with fury all over his face.

He fought back, shoving the younger man off him, rolling to the left so he could get back to his feet. He could feel the rushing flow of his blood as rage swept through him.

He was about to lunge back to his friend's brother when Nick came flying through the door toward the fight.

Nick tried to grab Charles, but his younger brother was slippery. He slid around Nick and went for Blaze again.

"You can't have her, she's mine!" Charles cried as he swung another fist at Blaze, hitting him in the stomach. Tears of anger made his eyes with an eerie light.

"She's not something...you...can...own!" Blaze yelled back as he delivered a few of his own blows to Charles's abdomen.

The younger man took the hits like they were nothing. He stood straight up and swung at Blaze again.

Blaze backed up just enough to miss the punch and return a right cross.

With a sickening crack, Charles's nose broke and blood spurted.

Nick grabbed his still struggling brother and pulled him a few feet from his friend.

"Hold him, Nick!" Blaze shouted. He came closer, his hands still in fists, ready to dish out a few more hits.

"Damn it! Stop, you two! This isn't high school!" Grace came closer to the three men, stepping in the way. She put one hand on both their chests, and took a deep breath, puffing it out. "Charles, how could you?"

He didn't look at her; his eyes were locked on Blaze, absolute fury burning in his hazel eyes. "Why do you have to take everything of mine?" Charles shouted at Blaze over Grace's shoulder.

Nick shifted in front of Grace to block Charles and looked down at his little brother, who was only a couple of inches shorter than him. "Dude what're you talking about?" he demanded, getting right in his brother's face.

"You and your stupid band; they took everything! Even the woman I love. It's never enough. He had to go and..." Charles wiped some of the blood off of his face and looked at Grace, now wrapped in Blaze's arms. "Why wasn't I enough for you? Not famous enough, not rich enough, not tough enough?"

Charles didn't wait for an answer. He stormed off into the building. The gathered crowd parted to make way for him.

"Are you okay?" Blaze wiped her tears away.

"Are *you* okay?"

"Psht. That was nothing." He shrugged one shoulder and one corner of his mouth shot up. "I'm sorry about that. So can I have that dance now?" The pressure throbbing in one eye told him it was swelling. Blaze's ears were ringing, and he tasted blood on his lips.

Grace wiped at some of it. His face would be swollen, even if he was playing the tough guy. "I think we better get you cleaned up first."

"Ah, a little blood never hurt anyone."

She wrapped her arms around his neck and rested her head on his shoulder.

He swayed, and she moved with him. The music had started again; the sound just barely tinkered outside, but it was enough to dance by.

"I'd be honored to dance with you." Grace slipped her hand into his and he spun her out once, pulling her back into his body. He could feel her heartbeat when they came back together.

His was still pounding hard from the adrenaline of the fight.

"We should go inside and take a look at your face," she said.

"I'm fine. But now I understand why you didn't want to see me again. It wasn't your schedule or even that other guy; it was Charles." Blaze pulled her a little closer, their cheeks now touching.

"It was all of the above. But I'm still scared," Grace confessed.

"You have nothing to fear with me. I will not hurt you." He could only hope she could tell how sincere he was.

"I know, but it doesn't stop it from being there."

$$\text{\clef treble} \, \flat \, \eighthnote \, \quarternote$$

CHARLES HELD a wad of napkins to his nose. He was in the car, and his brother drove him to the hospital. He was now cold-stone sober. He wished he wasn't. How had he let things get this far?

He'd been sitting at the bar, downing another drink. It was the fourth…or fifth? It didn't matter. The alcohol hadn't helped.

He couldn't stop seeing *his* Grace in Blaze's arms. Her body pressed against another man.

Charles had watched her arrival, the slinky green dress showing off all her curves, bringing his body alive. He'd planned to get her alone at some point, to show her they were meant to be.

Grace hadn't even notice him. She'd walked right into another man's arms. His brother's best friend. Blaze. He already had enough reasons to hate him. This was just one more.

Charles had ordered another drink.

"I think you've had enough," the bartender said.

"If I wanted your opinion, I'd ask for it. Pour me another."

As the older man turned to get the bottle from the shelf behind him, Charles had seen Grace head to the bathroom. She'd looked upset.

Good. Maybe he pissed her off. She'll see. Grace will know we are meant to be.

She'd told him no; that she didn't feel the same way about him, but he *loved* her. She'd see it. If he fought for her.

He gulped his new drink. The fire of the liquor fueled him. He shook the glass, listening to the ice *tink* against the glass.

Charles set the glass down when she came out of the ladies' room and followed Blaze out to the veranda.

He had had enough. He downed the entire drink, slammed the glass on the counter and jumped up. Charles had ripped Grace from Blaze's arms and threw a punch to the man's left cheek. He would've fought longer, had he not been torn away from the bastard.

"Charles, how could you?" would haunt him forever.

The tears on her cheeks. The hurt in her expression.

Because of *him*.

Nothing he'd ever wanted.

Charles needed her to want him. To need him like he needed her.

Love me back.

This was all wrong.

CHARLES GRABBED a pile of napkins off the bar after he'd fled the balcony; trying not to drip blood as he rode the elevator down to the lobby and headed outside the hotel. He didn't know where to go. Walking made him feel better. Sometimes he could walk for hours. His head hurt.

So did his soul.

"Charles?"

He hadn't expected to hear his brother's voice.

"Go away," he threw over his shoulder.

"Charles, come back. We need to get you taken care of," Nick said, placing a hand on his shoulder.

"Why? You don't give a damn about me. You don't care! You never have!" He shouted as he pivoted to face his brother.

"How can you say that?" Nick asked, hurt in his question.

"It's true and you know it. You were gone the whole time we were growing up. You care more about your precious *Razor's Edge* than you do about your own family."

"That's not true." Now his brother was defensive.

"Really? Then why didn't you come to Barbara's funeral?" He asked. It would be a thrown dagger in his brother's chest.

"There's more to that and you know it," Nick sounded deceptively calm.

"You didn't love her. You didn't even come to say goodbye." Charles wanted his brother to hurt as much as he did.

"I loved her just as much as you. And you're right, I should've made it. I just...I couldn't deal with it, dude. How do you bury your little sister? It was my job to protect her, to protect all of you, and instead I was flying around the world." He took a breath that made his chest heave. "I fucked up, okay? Is that what you want to hear? I feel guilty, but I can't change that. Barb knows how much I loved her. I dedicated the rest of my tour to her. What more do you want from me?"

"I want my big brother back." The truth fell out of his mouth in a whisper.

Nick pulled Charles into a fierce hug. "I'm here, Chucky. I'll always be here."

. . .

CHARLES STILL COULDN'T BELIEVE his brother stayed with him when they set his nose. That'd hurt more than Blaze breaking it. By the time they left, he looked like he'd just had a rhinoplasty. Complete with splinting. It hurt like a bitch.

"I think you should go stay at my place for a while," Nick said.

"Nashville? What the hell am I gonna do in NashVegas?"

His brother laughed at the nickname the city he lived in had been branded. "Well, try not to drink too much. Those meds are gonna kick your ass if you add liquor to them. Angel's there right now. Spend some time with her. She misses you."

Charles didn't want to spend time with his twin sister. He wanted to go see Grace and fix things. He swallowed a sigh.

After what'd happened, neither his brother, nor Blaze, would let him get anywhere near her.

He'd have to bide his time.

Charles sat in the hotel room his brother had insisted he get for him, looking down at the printed airline ticket Nick had taken care of when they checked in, and his mind was whirling with ideas.

You can't have her, Blaze. You and her were never meant to be. She wants me.

CHAPTER 13

L IGHTNING ARCHED AND LIT UP THE SKY. G RACE STEPPED BACK OUT to the double glass doors onto the balcony after cleaning up Blaze's bloodied face and hands.

Blaze had his back to her, his hands on the railing. He was looking over the cityscape. He was backlit by Mother Nature's light show.

All she wanted to do was run into his arms, but she enjoyed the view. She took each step slowly and struggled with a difficult decision.

The night was a perfect temperature, not too hot, not too cool, with a hint of humidity as they waited for the rain.

Grace inhaled, letting the scents fill her as she reached him and touched his shoulder.

Her heart melted. She'd never seen such joy on anyone's face before.

How did I get so lucky to have someone like him look at me like this? Maybe I can do this and not end up a tragic tale like my parents. Is it worth the risk?

She slid her hands over his shoulders to wrap around his neck and laced her fingers to lock him in.

Blaze opened his mouth but she robbed him of his words before he could speak.

His hot breath filled her, sending a fire raging through her body.

His hands had gone to her waist, then moved to the small of her back, to ever so gently pull her in closer to him.

As their tongues did a seductive dance, and their bodies melded perfectly together, the sky opened up.

Their kiss broke and Grace giggled. The rain came down on them. It was still warm and their clothing stuck to them.

He ran the back of his knuckles along her cheek. "I could make love to you right here, in this rain." His voice was thick with lust.

"That's not such a good idea. There're people in the other room," Grace teased, glancing over her shoulder to the ballroom filled with the people she'd spent the last five months with.

He didn't reply, instead, he kissed her with a fervor she wasn't expecting. "All I want to do right now is peel you out of your clothes and enjoy your beautiful body. But you don't have a room to yourself. I'm not about to shared you with three other women." He grabbed her hand and her laughter trail behind them as they ran into the building.

"Where are we going?" Grace asked.

Blaze dragged her toward the front desk, rather than toward the exit. "To get a room."

"But, don't you have one nearby?"

His hotel had to be close; they'd walked to it from the bar the night before, but Grace had been too drunk to remember where it was.

"It's too far. I want you…now."

At the front desk, Blaze smiled at the guy who was attending.

Grace's cheeks flushed hot because he spoke in a rush.

"Do you have any rooms available for tonight? I don't care what size, or how much. I just need a room. I need it now."

They were both soaking wet, their clothes sticking to their skin.

No doubt, the front desk clerk could see right through her green dress, because his cheeks were just as red as hers.

He nodded.

Blaze pulled his wallet out and slapped a credit card on the counter.

The clerk handed over the key. "Thank you, Mr. Solan."

Blaze grabbed her hand and tugged her down the hallway.

Grace laughed again. "Any idea what room we're in?" Giggles racked her frame.

"Oh yeah, I guess it is important, isn't it?" He dropped her hand and ran back to the counter.

Grace shook her head in disbelief as he hurried back to her, but she couldn't stop smiling.

"We're in 740," he panted, and hurried them to the elevator.

It was a good thing she hadn't had that drink.

This would be a night Grace would never forget.

Blaze hadn't cared what kind of room they got, and neither did she.

They found out together, the moment they opened the door, which was at the end of the hall.

Blaze opened the door and flipped the light switch on, then moved to the side to allow her to step in first.

The room took her breath away.

Apparently, it was a suite.

Her heart fluttered at the beauty of it. It'd clearly been styled with Old Hollywood in mind. The walls were a stunning mint color, the furniture a beautiful warm wood, like cherry. To the right was a tall rolling top writing desk and across from that was the king sized bed with white linen, trimmed in gold.

Grace looked passed the luxury of the room to glance at the

open ivory gauze curtains that led to a veranda. It was still raining but it was such a beautiful sound.

Blaze stepped up behind her and slid his hand across the slippery fabric of her wet dress to incase her waist. His warm lips kissed her cold right shoulder.

A delicious shiver danced down her spine.

It feels like I am making the right decision. Please, let me not screw this up.

♪

BLAZE HELD his breath when they walked into the room. He'd hoped for something nice. His worries about getting stuck with something crappy were unfounded. The suite was awesome.

A great way to make an impression.

Although, Grace wasn't the type that needed to be impressed.

She cared about Blaze. She didn't even know who BJ was.

It lightened his heart.

Blaze stepped up behind her. The light green material of her dress was clinging to all her curves, in all the right ways. The dress was ruined; no doubt it was dry-clean only.

When they'd been on the patio in the rain, his body had stirred with one look at her. As if she'd been standing there naked.

He hadn't complained when the front desk attendant hadn't been able to speak. How could he with the beauty of Grace standing before him?

Not that he wanted another man to look at her, even that obvious nerd.

Her bare shoulder was calling to him. Blaze slid his hands across the wet material and left one hand on her stomach, with the other on her hip. He dipped down to kiss her shoulder. Grace's skin was cold, but that one little touch of his lips heated them both.

She turned in his arms to face him, lust filling her eyes. They were green, vivid green, and matching her gown. They hadn't appeared this green earlier.

She closed the objects of his fascination and moved closer in slow-motion.

Their lips met and passion exploded.

Blaze couldn't help himself; his hands moved of their own accord. Within seconds, Grace's dress was a wet puddle around her ankles. He grabbed her arm so she could take a step out and come back to him.

Her fingers worked to peel his wet clothing from him and soon enough they both stood in only their damp underwear.

Grace laughed.

He reached for her, pulling her close, if nothing else to warm her up. He took her mouth again, and things rose to a fevered pitch. Roving caresses joined the show; no inch of skin went untouched.

They moved toward the massive king-sized bed. The backs of her legs collided with the mattress and he stopped her from falling. She giggled against his lips and plopped down on the edge of the bed.

His chuckled and gently pushed her backward.

Blaze climbed on the bed and straddled her, looking down into her beautiful eyes.

They hadn't said a word since they'd entered the suite, and he didn't want to break the magical spell wrapped around them.

He leaned down and kissed her forehead, followed by her cheeks, and last, her lips.

Grace raked her hands across his back and their kissing continued.

His entire body was likely to go up in flames. The painful pleasure of her nails on sensitive skin was new. He scooted her up the bed so her head was on the pillows, and her long legs could stretch out.

He would spend the entire night enjoying every inch of her body. She'd been hurt and he wanted to make things better.

Blaze hovered above to nibble at her neck and she had her hands on his back, just under his arms.

She moved her legs, bending her right. With a little momentum, she flipped their positions, surprising him, and leaving her on top.

Her hair came undone after being in the rain, and it was drying and frizz out. Tresses fell forward as she bent to kiss him. It tickled his chest and he gave her more of a laugh than a kiss.

He grabbed her hips when she rocked against him. "You're killing me," he whispered. Blaze hooked his thumbs into her barely-there white satin and lace panties, and she lifted so he could shimmy them down.

He explored so much of her as she'd hovered over him. More than once he'd foreseen her climax. He slid his fingers up and down her inner thigh, and her skin quivered beneath his touch.

Grace lowered her hips and he could feel her heat pressing against his tip.

He tried not to buck up, and let her be in control. Blaze clenched his teeth to steady himself as she slowly brought herself onto him, taking all of him in.

She rode him, the rhythm was perfect, and he met her along the way.

He held her hips to help her thrust, and she threw her head back, riding him hard.

She bit her lip as she drove down harder. Her body tightened around him as she climaxed.

She's a screamer.

Blaze was so revved up, he needed a distraction. He wasn't ready to be done yet. This was just the beginning; he wanted to spend the entire night making love to her.

Grace almost collapsed on his chest as she succumbed to the exhaustion of an orgasm.

He kissed the closest shoulder and she buried her face in the mattress next to his head. Her lithe body convulsed around him as an aftershock rocked her. He flipped them without dislodging from her body. He moved so he was completely over her.

Grace gasped, and slid her long legs around his waist.

His hands landed on either side of her head. He swooped down to capture her mouth. He couldn't stop touching her, tasting her.

He inhaled, becoming intoxicated by the scent of their love-making. He thrust hard, driving them higher on the bed.

She cried out again and her sex tightened around his. He bit back a groan to keep himself from coming right then.

Grace's legs tightened around him and it would be his doom.

She panted and moaned with each thrust, bringing him even closer to his release. It was still coming too fast.

"Let's try something," he whispered, pulling out of her gently.

Grace just blinked, then nodded.

Blaze urged her up on all fours. He'd usually taken his girl-friends this way, so he didn't have to face them.

That wasn't the case with Grace.

Everything had been different and he wanted to see if this would be, too.

Grace reached between her legs and helped to guide Blaze back in. She gasped as he entered her.

She'd been noisy before; this was a whole new level.

"Oh my God, oh my God," she panted, like a mantra. "Harder Blaze, harder!" Grace called.

He obliged. His climax built back, even more intense than before. His spine tingled and his balls were heavy.

No, not like this.

Blaze didn't want to end it this way, like all the other girls. He wanted to see her face.

He pulled out and patted her hip. "Roll back over," he whispered again. "I need to see you."

Grace smiled, and she looked deep into his eyes. She opened her arms and invited him back into her body.

He could have sworn he saw the same thing in her eyes.

She wanted to watch him as he came, too.

He wished he could've taken her over the edge once more, but just looking into her green eyes had been all Blaze needed for that final push.

He cried out and shuddered as his orgasm shot deep.

It was his turn to collapse onto Grace.

CHAPTER 14

GRACE COULD LIVE TO BE A HUNDRED AND TEN AND STILL WOULD never forget his beauty. It wasn't just in his appearance, although that was fabulous on its own; it was the way he made her feel, and how he looked after her. She traced her fingertips up and down his tattoos.

What her parents had shared wasn't just fairy tales. Intense passion was real, and worth loosing sleep over. She was finally ready to tell him about her mother. She needed the right moment to tell Blaze.

Will it turn him away from me? If he knows the truth?

Her body shook, whether from getting cold, coming down from the fire they'd created, or the fear she now had; she couldn't narrow it down.

Blaze perched himself up on his elbows. "How about a shower to warm us up?"

"That would be fabulous!"

He'd wrapped her in one of the soft plush robes behind the bathroom door, and they waited for the water in the shower to be the right temperature. His back was to her and he checked the heat.

She bit her lip as she looked him over again, now with new eyes. Grace bit her lip. She was sober and clear thinking.

Oddly enough, shoulder blades on a man were a hot spot for her, and *his* were her cup of tea. There were defined muscles, not too built up, showing he must workout.

Her eyes traveled lower.

His ass had the perfect curve to the cheeks. She wanted to reach out and touch him. Before, she'd cupped that ass as he'd made love to her.

Don't squeeze the Charmin...

She snickered to herself. Grace's cheeks flushed with heat when he whirled, and caught her staring.

"Water's ready."

He'd let her step in first and always made sure she stayed as close to the hot water, so she wouldn't get colder.

She laughed when he tickled her with the washcloth, washing her body for her.

"I'm a big girl and can wash myself."

"The way I see it, I got you dirty, it's my job to get you clean," Blaze insisted. He turned her body around, giving him access to her back.

She placed her hands on the tiled wall when he caressed her with the soapy cloth. She moaned in pleasure as his hands massaged the muscles in her shoulders, working out knots she didn't know she had.

He continued lower, applying pressure in all the right places.

Grace was putty in his hands.

He slid his hands around her waist, encouraging her to turn again.

What was that look in his dark eyes?

It couldn't be lust; she knew what that looked like, and this wasn't it.

Neither was it the way her father had looked at her mother.

Her lack of experience left her unsure of… everything.

He broke her thought by bringing the washcloth back into play. He once again started at her shoulders, working his way down. He tenderly fondled one breast, then the other, making sure every inch of her was clean.

Blaze left a trail of heat down her stomach as he moved lower. Dropping the washcloth, he replaced it with his bare hand, seeking her most sensitive spot. He separated her folds, and slipped a finger inside her.

Grace gasped. Her breathing came hard and fast.

He teased her body, bringing it once again to life.

She had to grip his shoulders to keep standing, her knees suddenly weak as the intense tingling began. "Oh… oh…. Oh…" She dug her nails into his shoulders and convulsed from the orgasm. "Oh my God, I am so sorry," she said, running her fingertips over the marks she'd left.

"Don't worry. They were worth it."

It had to be after three am when they left the bathroom, and they were both exhausted. Grace wouldn't have minded making love again, but neither of them had it in them.

She wrapped herself in the robe again and moved to sit on the edge of the bed while Blaze took their wet clothing and hung it over the shower curtain rod, hoping they'd have something to wear by morning.

She could've snuck to her room on the fifth floor, and gotten fresh clothes, but then she'd have to deal with her roommates. Right now she had something more important to deal with.

Blaze returned to her, weariness written across his face. His eyes were heavy and he tried to stifle a yawn.

I'll tell him tomorrow.

🎵

GRACE WOKE to find her body deliciously sore. She'd never

known she could feel so good. Not just physically, but emotionally, spiritually.

Blaze had his arms wrapped around her and her head rested on his hard chest. His heart beat steadily beneath her palm. She tilted her head ever so slightly to look at the clock on the nightstand.

Oh, shit!

It was already ten in the morning. She was due to meet Jason and Richard at the new theater at 11:30 a.m..

She wanted to stay right where she was; her future, but another big piece of her future was waiting outside the door.

I still need to have that talk with him... oh God, that sounds bad! I'll do it later...

Grace didn't want to wake him, so she carefully slipped from his arms and slid off the bed. The soft white robe she'd worn the night before still lay discarded on the floor. She picked it up and enveloped herself in its warmth, not looking forward to putting on her cold dress. Grace was headed to the bathroom when she heard his soft sweet voice.

"You're not trying to sneak away from me again are you?"

She stuck her head around the corner and smiled at him. "No, I'm not sneaking out. But I gotta go. I need to get ready to meet up with the company owner and our new benefactor."

"You could take a shower here." His voice was husky and full of seduction, but with an undertone of exhaustion.

"I heard the showers here have a two person occupancy. I'm afraid if I took you up on that offer, I'd never leave this room. And my future would be in jeopardy."

He laughed with her before he curled his finger, indicating for her to come closer. "At least give me a kiss good morning, to tide me over until I see you this afternoon."

It was dangerous to go back to him but she agreed; she could use a kiss to get her through the day. She went to the edge of the bed, the front of her knees against the box springs. Grace leaned forward, reaching for him so she could slip her hands around his neck.

Instead of just kissing her, Blaze wrapped his arms around her and flipped her onto the bed.

She landed on her back beside him.

He swiftly straddled her, his hands on either side of her head. His kiss was soft and sweet, followed by a little laugh against her lips. "One way or another, I got you back in my bed."

"Ouch," she said. "That hurts. Is that the only reason you're keeping me around?" She was joking but the happy look on his face dissolved.

He sat back on his heels and was careful not to crush her legs. Blaze let out a deep sigh as he ran his knuckle along her jawline. "Grace, I'm not that other guy. I'm not going to use you and then discard you. From the first time I saw you I knew I needed you in my life. I…"

She didn't let him finish. She crushed his words with a fiery kiss.

Grace would be late for her meeting.

CHAPTER 15

BLAZE HUNG OUT WITH NICK AND HOPE WHILE GRACE WAS AT HER meeting. It was nice to see his buddy interested in a girl worth his time.

He'd picked them up at the hotel in his red Mustang convertible. "So, what do you wanna see?" he asked Hope as they climbed in the car.

"Well, I've never been to L.A., so what ever you think would be fun."

"Oh, honey, just spending time with Blaze and I is fun," Nick teased.

Blaze drove around town, the hot August air blown over his face, and whipping everyone's hair around. He was grateful Hope didn't asked to have the top up. He didn't think he'd be able to oblige. He was on the road with the band more often than not, and rarely drove around town. The day was almost perfect.

Nick pointed out various places their band had performed, as the car sped down the road. Pride showed in his voice when he spoke about *Razor's Edge.*

Not that he wasn't proud of his life, but Blaze was glad he didn't feel the need to brag about it to Grace.

She didn't care.

They pulled into the parking lot of a museum.

"Um, where are we?" Hope asked when Nick helped her out of the back seat.

"La Brea Tar Pits. Blaze likes come see where he deposited some of his ex-girlfriends."

He glared at his best friend. Of course, Nick didn't know where he and Grace stood, but making comments like that in front of *her* best friend was uncalled for.

"I thought we came here to visit *your* relatives." Instead of bitching him out, he gave it back.

"Whatever bro, you're the one that was driving. You picked the place. Come on, Hope. Let's go check out the museum."

Blaze stood there a moment and watched them walk away. What he wouldn't have given to have Grace by his side to enjoy the warm day. Even though she was doing something far more important.

Changing her life.

They walked around the tar pits, checking out the sculptures before lingering inside the museum, watching a team clean fossils.

Every so often, he glanced over his shoulder. Tingles up and down his spine convinced him someone was watching him. Since he was in a very famous pop group, he was easily recognized.

In L.A. he wasn't bothered by fans often, but the rare occasion had happened. So when in he was out in public, Blaze was always on alert.

No one came forward, but the uneasiness didn't dissipate.

Hope was walking slowly, clearly wearing out when he checked his watch for the tenth time.

"It's almost one. Grace said she'd meet us for lunch. Maybe we should head that way?"

"Sounds good! I am starving," her bestie admitted.

Blaze drove them to an old movie theater called *The Majestic*.

It didn't look like it'd been a working theater in years. The front was covered with semi-clear plastic torn in various places. The very old-looking marquee had multiple busted light bulbs, but the name of the place was still visible.

"What're we doing here?" Nick asked, distain marring his voice.

"Picking Grace up. I thought we'd surprise her." Blaze smiled his devilish grin.

Hope smiled back conspiratorially.

The outside of the old theater gave the impression that renovations were slow-going, but as his eyes adjusted to the indoor lighting, Blaze recognized they were going for its original glory. It *was* majestic.

He let his gaze roam the lobby. Where was everyone? Or anyone? No one had jumped on them, ordering them out. Blaze could hear voices; one was Grace's laughter.

All four sets of double doors were open, leading into the theater.

Blaze held his breath as they walked into the spacious auditorium.

The seats had all been re-covered in stunning burgundy velour and beautiful gold trim accented the lights and balcony. It was a theater from old movies. He was standing in such a gorgeous image from the past.

Hope went down to the front row and sat in the center seat.

Blaze and Nick followed, taking seats on either side of her.

"Oh no, you two!" Hope pushed them out of their seats. "I'm here to see a play, so go entertain me."

Nick flashed a naughty smile and ran toward stage right.

Hope raised an eyebrow in Blaze's direction.

"Why do we both gotta go? Nick's a solo artist, he doesn't need me," he jokingly complained, trying to get out.

"I believe you are, too," she replied.

He tilted his head in surprise. Didn't speak.

"Yes, I downloaded your solo album this morning, too. Now get up there." Hope pushed him up and out of his seat.

He groaned at headed stage left.

Nick climbed up on a ladder that had been left in the orchestra pit, leaning on the stage. "Romeo, Romeo where art thou, Romeo?" His question was high-pitched, squeaky voice, his right hand on his chest over his heart, as his left held tight on the ladder.

"Really, Dude? Romeo and Juliet?" Blaze laughed.

A huge grin spread across Nick's face.

"Come on, Blaze!" Hope called. "Do a little Shakespeare for me!"

Blaze transformed before. His badass demeanor melted away, and Romeo stood on stage. "'But soft, what light through yonder window breaks? It is the east and Juliet is the sun! Arise fair sun and kill the envious moon, Who is already sick and pale with grief. That thou her maid art far more fair than she.'"

GRACE HAD a hard time focusing throughout her very important meeting. Blaze was still on her mind, and his scent all over her.

It wasn't until the two men were talking directly to her, as opposed to building permit and merger stuff, that she could pay attention.

"Grace? Grace? Are you paying attention?" Jason, her manager, asked.

"She's just mesmerized by my beauty," Richard, the theater's owner teased.

She laughed to cover her embarrassment. Hoped like hell her cheeks weren't bright pink. Thank God they couldn't read her mind.

When Jason had told her they wanted her to become a permanent part of the company, Grace thought that meant as an actress. That part was true, but they were offering her so much more.

Richard had been so impressed with how she'd gotten him to sign with the company, he wanted her to be the PR for the theater, and Jason agreed she should do the same for the company.

The position proposed when she wasn't on stage or rehearsing, she'd be schmoozing with all the big time people, getting more funding help and promoting the company.

They wanted her to start right away.

"I still have my apartment in Denver. I'll need time to find somewhere in L.A. to live, and get packed up and moved. I need… at least two weeks."

She was surprised and flattered when Richard offered her a townhome in a building he owned. She wanted to jump on it, but worried her tight actor's budget wouldn't be able to afford it.

"We'll work it out with your salary," he'd said.

Grace protested, but the man held up a hand to silence her.

They agreed to give her just under two weeks. She'd start her new job, at the theater that following Monday. That left her with only a few days to get to Denver and get packed.

As excited as she was, Grace's heart twisted. Was she ready to let her past go and move forward?

She'd be leaving the last place she'd seen her parents alive. She wouldn't get to visit their gravestones, or eat at their favorite restaurants.

Grace would be starting a new life.

If I'm to have any chance of packing all my stuff, I have to leave tomorrow.

That left her with a week to pack, and four days to drive half way across the country.

Can I pack it all up in a week? Should I tell Blaze, or wait and see if he even still cares after we have our 'talk'?

· · ·

GRACE STOOD JUST outside the office; she swore she could hear his voice. She followed the sounds to the auditorium.

Hope sat in the front row.

Nick was perched on a little ladder leaning against the stage.

Blaze slowly climbed the steps.

Nick quoted Romeo and Juliet.

Oh, how she knew this play so well.

Grace ran around to the left side entrance, where the stairs led to the upper balcony. She opened the door ever so careful, inched close to the edge to see Blaze recite his lines.

Her lover was looking right at Nick, who was still standing on the ladder.

She waved to Nick and put her finger on her lips to shush him.

He nodded as Blaze continued Romeo's lines.

> "'As daylight doth a lamp. Her eyes in heaven.
> Would through the airy region stream so bright
> that birds would sing and think it not night. See
> how she leans her cheek upon her hand. O, that I
> were that glove upon that hand. That I might
> touch that cheek.'"

"*Aye me,*" Grace cried out.

Blaze whirled around, a smile lighting his face when she stepped onto the balcony.

> "'She speaks. O, speak again, bright angel, for thou
> art as glorious to this night, being o'er my head,
> as a winged messenger of heaven. Unto the
> white up-turned wondering eyes, Of mortals
> that fall back to gaze on him when he bestrides
> the lazy-puffing clouds and sails upon the
> bosom of air.'"

Grace brought her hands together and up to her chest before continuing.

> "'O, Romeo, Romeo! Wherefore art thou Romeo?
>   Deny thy father and refuse thy name; or, if thou
>   wilt not, be but sworn my love, and I'll no longer
>   be a Capule*t*.'"

The auditorium filled with applause.

Not just Hope and Nick, but Richard, Jason, and a few of the construction men.

Grace's cheeks flushed red-hot. She ran from the balcony, almost falling down the stairs in her hurry to join her friends.

"And *this* is why she is our star," Jason bragged to one of the men.

More heat suffused her face and neck. She smiled through it and worked her way past them to get to Blaze.

He opened his arms and welcomed her home as she stepped onto the stage. "That was fun."

"I can't believe you knew all of that!" Grace grinned through her surprise. "That was a long piece and you didn't falter at all."

"There was a time in my life when I needed to keep myself busy. So I read a lot. Shakespeare has always fascinated me. Romeo and Juliet is such a great and tragic story." He kissed the top of her head.

"Well, I'm impressed."

Blaze beamed. "High praise from an awesome actor."

Grace grinned and her tummy flipped. Having his respect made him even more attractive. "Are you ready to go get lunch?" Grace asked. Her tummy rumbled.

"Not yet. Nick and I have one thing we need to do first."

Nick, who nodded and came on stage. "Why don't you come up here, Hope? Grace, stay put!"

The guys exchanged a look, then Blaze sang.

"The moment I met you, my beauty, my life as I
    knew it, had changed.
You gave me your back, denied your broken heart,
Even it deserves a second chance."

Nick took over then.

"Just a minute of your time, that's all I'm asking for,
    to show you what you mean to me."

Blaze sang alone again,

"Don't put us all together, not all men are created
    the same."

They sang the next part together.

"Let me mend your broken heart, let me wipe your
    tears,
My life is tied to yours, we've waited all these years.
Let me mend your broken heart, let me wipe your
    tears.
My life is tied to yours, we've waited all these years."

THEY ENDED with an unbelievable harmonic tone.

Grace threw her arms around Blaze and kissed him as if they were alone. It would've been a seriously romantic moment, but her stomach had to ruin it with a huge ghastly rumble.

"Sounds like we need to feed you," he teased.

She grinned. "Yes, please."

CHAPTER 16

GRACE'S HAIR BLEW IN ALL DIRECTIONS AS THEY DROVE WITH THE top down through the streets of Los Angeles.

Nick and Hope sat in the back of Blaze's Mustang. Occasionally she heard Hope laugh behind her. No doubt, Nick was doing something to her friend.

She rested her hand on Blaze's upper thigh.

He had one hand on the steering wheel and one on the gearshift.

She *had* to keep touching him to keep the sadness of leaving soon at bay. She'd see him again; she was moving to L.A. after all.

He pulled into the parking lot of a little Asian restaurant. The aroma from inside was drifting out as customers opened the front door.

She was so hungry; she didn't care where they ate.

Blaze put the car in park and hit a switch so the soft top moved into place.

THEY LAUGHED and talked as they sat at the table, each sipping a green tea and waiting for their food.

Grace was normally the loud and outgoing one, yet she found herself afraid to speak.

Blaze put his hand on her thigh and smiled before he spoke. "Is everything okay, baby?" His brow was drawn tight. He was concerned.

"Yeah," she said. "It's just…" Words wouldn't come.

"Did things not go well at the meeting? It sounded like you were happy."

"Yeah, it was great." She took a deep breath. "They want me to start at this new job in two weeks."

"That's wonderful, Grace! I have a feeling you will fit right in L.A.," Nick said.

"Except… I know I'm on a month to month lease, but I'm still worried they need more notice I'm vacating."

"Seriously? Aren't you always complaining about not knowing you neighbors because the turn around is so high? I doubt that's gonna be a problem."

"I need to figure out a budget. Moving is expensive and I'm not…" She put her hand over her mouth.

"Oh," Blaze said. "That's what you're concerned about?"

"No."

"I can—"

She held up a hand to silence him. "I've got this. I just need to work through a few things."

"All right, baby. When do you leave?"

Grace didn't miss the tender word he'd just called her. It was sweet, endearing. And it tore at her heart.

Will he still call me that after I sit him down tonight and have that chat?

"I have to leave tomorrow morning. I'm rather quick at packing, it's the drive that's gonna kill me."

"Why don't you just get someone else to pack for you," Nick suggested.

"I learned from a young age not to let someone else pack for you. Things get broken, or stolen. If I pack it and break it, it's my own damn fault."

"I can come with you and help you pack," Blaze said.

"Umm. No, you can't," Nick said. "Wednesday and Friday we're filming shows remember? Ellen and Jimmy Kimmel? Management would kick your ass if you disappeared. The Ellen show is her once a year anything-goes live show. We can't *not* have you there."

"Dammit!" he cursed under his breath.

"It's okay, I'm better at packing when I'm alone, anyway. I just turn on some music and get it done."

"Have you moved a lot?" Blaze asked.

"I'm a military brat."

"Do I need to worry about your father coming to hunt me down with a shotgun?" Her lover teased.

Grace lowered her head, trying not to let the tears start flowing. "No. My parents are deceased. I'm all alone. So there's no one you have to worry about."

"Grace, I'm so sorry. Why didn't you tell me?" Blaze was crestfallen, and she couldn't be mad at him. He had no way of knowing, of course.

I'm still afraid to tell you to whole *truth...*

AFTER LUNCH, Blaze took them back to the hotel.

She grabbed his hand while they were still by the car. "Wait just a moment?"

"What is it?"

Nick and Hope went inside, giving them a moment of privacy.

"There is something I need to talk to you about." She took a breath.

"Don't worry, Grace. I know you're nervous about moving.

Who wouldn't be; L.A. is a big change from Denver. But honey, you got me to show you around town. We got this."

If only it were that simple...

Nick and Hope were waiting for them in the lobby.

Blaze took her hand and kissed her knuckles. "Hey, Nick? Can Grace and I meet back up with you two for dinner? I want to help prepare her for her move into L.A., and show her some stuff on my laptop."

His buddy chuckled. "Show her stuff on your laptop? That's the first time I've ever heard you talk about sex like that."

Grace's face went hot. She'd believed Blaze—she could use the pointers—but sex would be nice, too.

No! I need to get this out!

"Seriously, dude? Is that all you ever think about? Wait, don't answer that. I don't wanna embarrass Hope."

Her friend wore a grateful smile, but her cheeks were pink. Hope had always been shy.

"Should we meet you here in the lobby, say seven-thirty?" Nick asked.

"Sounds great, thanks, bro."

Grace looked over her shoulder at and winked at Hope, as Blaze dragged her toward the elevators, but they both smiled.

Blaze opened the door and she stepped into the suite.

His suitcase standing next to the dresser. The last time she'd had been in this room, the only thing he had was the clothes on his back, which had ended up on the floor, soaking wet. She arched an eyebrow and shot him a glance.

He'd followed her gaze. "When you left me to go get ready for your meeting, I went over to my other hotel, packed up, and checked out. My house is only about an hour from here if there's no traffic, but it just seemed easier to get a hotel room the other night."

"If I'm gonna stay the night with you, we should go get my things, too."

She'd always been OCD about keeping her belongings organized and mostly packed so when it was time to move to the next town, she was already prepared to go. So Grace had little to do this time.

Blaze stood at the door, waiting for her to hand something to him.

"Are you sure you can carry all this? We can call downstairs for a trolley."

"I got this, babe. Just pile it on."

She handed him a giant suitcase, her laptop bag, and an enormous garment bag. Grace went into the bathroom to grab her makeup and toiletries. On top of the train case she kept them in, was a red rose. She peeked out into the bedroom, checking for the previous roses. Both flowers lay in front of the tv, darkening as they dried out.

Why does Maxine keep setting them here? They must belong to one of the other girls. Everybody knows I hate roses.

She dropped it on the counter, picked up her things and joined Blaze.

HER HEART WAS light as they stepped back into his suite, all her things in their arms. Grace hung the garment bag in the closet next to his wrinkled clothing. She could swear they still looked wet.

"Have a seat on the bed, babe and I'll pull out my laptop so I can show you maps of L.A.."

Her heart slammed and she grabbed her own computer bag.

Should I let him help me out before I drop the news? Damn it! I should've told him before we got my stuff!

She pulled out her device. She'd seen her most recently opened bag of Reese's Pieces tucked in there. She needed to check her email, even if he planned to use his own laptop to show her around.

Jason was supposed to send Grace her flight info for Denver.

She balanced her machine on her knees, sitting crisscrossed in the middle of the bed, with her Reese's Pieces between her legs, and waiting for Blaze to join her. She shoved a handful of candy in her mouth.

He laughed.

"Whath tho fummy?" Grace asked through a mouthful.

"Wow, babe. We just finished lunch and you are stuffing your face with candy?"

She flashed a goofy smile.

Blaze dove across the bed, knocking her backward, her laptop fell beside her. He landed halfway-across her body.

It should've hurt, but it didn't.

The look in his eyes made her laugh, and she almost choked on the candy in her mouth.

"And this is why I dig you. You'll smile at me with candy in your face, which is so sexy. No Little Miss Proper for you."

Grace wrapped her arms around his neck, and kissed him so fiercely.

"Have I mentioned I have a peanut allergy?" Blaze asked.

She pulled away quickly. "Oh my God, are you serious? Are you going to be okay?" Her heart dropped to her toes, and her gut churned Reese's.

When Blaze laughed, Grace growled and smacked his chest.

"Hey! You really scared me! That wasn't nice!" She didn't focus on how his teasing made her contemplate how little she really knew about him.

He beamed, unrepentant. "Actually, Reese's is one of my favorite candies. Let me kiss you again and share the sweet flavor."

"Why should I let you, after that? Besides, I thought you were supposed to show me L.A. on the computer?"

"As my lady wishes." Blaze was true to his word to Nick; he sat up and apologized for his assault.

Grace pouted, making a little whiny noise. She hadn't expected him to take her up on her not-really-serious offer.

He smiled again, leaned over, and kissed her nose. "Later, baby. Promise."

Blaze opened his laptop.

Grace watched the screen come to light. Unfortunately, the computer wasn't the only thing turned on. "Richard offered me one of the townhomes he owns," she said, needing a distraction in a big way. She grabbed her cell; she'd made a note with the address he'd given her. "He said Tuesday morning he'll have a lease agreement, salary paperwork, and the keys to the new place overnighted, so I should have them by Wednesday." She reached for her laptop and Googled her new address. "Look, here it is."

Blaze grinned as he studied her screen. "Babe, our places are less than two miles apart."

Great. If he never speaks to me again, there's still a risk I'll run into him...

♪♩

"I STILL CAN'T BELIEVE Richard bought my flight. Looks like I leave at nine a.m. tomorrow morning. I'll get into Denver at 1:05 p.m."

Blaze helped her to get a U-Haul truck and car trailer reserved online. They ordered boxes and tape to be delivered to her house Tuesday afternoon.

"That gives me a little bit of tomorrow night to get started on packing. I'm worried I won't get everything done in a week. I'd hate to leave anything behind."

"If you have to leave anything behind, we can go back, finish packing it up and bring it back," he said.

She still couldn't believe such a wonderful guy had walked into her life. Grace glanced at the clock; it was already 6:45 p.m.

Where did the time go? I still haven't told him.

"So, what are the plans for tonight? After dinner with Nick and Hope?" she asked. She really needed to be done with this.

"We could just have dinner here in the hotel, make it quick and easy. My favorite place to go on Monday nights when I'm home, happens to be this tiny little dive bar that has karaoke tonight. Any interest in spending another night singing?"

Grace laughed. *Is he serious?* She loved to sing. Hell, that was her profession. It was his, too. She grinned. "You claim to be this big pop star, but you're gonna go to some dive bar and sing karaoke? I don't buy it."

"It's L.A., baby. Ain't nobody famous when everybody's famous." He chuckled. "It's a tiny place, kinda like Cheers, where everybody knows your name. It's one of the few places I can go and just be Blaze, not the pop star BJ."

She nodded, pretending like she understood. "I should change then." She was still dressed in her business casual outfit of slimming black slacks and a button up blouse with a cami underneath; what she'd picked for her meeting.

One more night. Give me one more night. I will *tell him...*

GRACE SELECTED a cute red halter that tied in the back. It was long enough to go to her hips, and she paired it with dark skinny-jeans and red pumps. It was sexy on a good day, but the clothes didn't matter. It was the way *he* looked at her.

It made her melt, and made her want to get naked and forget their plans.

The heels made her taller than her lover, and she would've worried about it—she towered over Blaze by a good four inches, but he seemed to love he was standing next to someone so tall.

She could just stare at him all night if he continued to look back the way he did.

It wasn't just sexual desire in his face, but something else, something more. Something that made heart hurt but her body tingle.

What am I going to do?

He'd changed as well, going with something a little more casual than the button up he'd had on earlier. He'd kept the same black faded jeans with a sparkly encrusted skull belt buckle.

Blaze had donned a black T-shirt with an image of vintage Popeye on it. Over it, he'd tossed on a red, black, and white plaid flannel with rolled up sleeves. His baseball cap was an ode to the Yankees.

She waited for him to add sunglasses like one always saw movie actors doing when they were trying to hide.

He never did.

DINNER WAS UNEVENTFUL, other than they all argued over who was paying for the meal.

Grace was so used to standing on her own two feet; it was hard to let anyone take care of her, even if it was just a dining bill. The guys won that battle, and soon enough they were walking into the bar.

"Will you sing something with me?" Blaze asked.

"I'd love to, but do we both know anything, other than songs from *Grease?*" she teased.

"We can look over Dave's books."

"Dave?" Hope asked.

"Yeah. He's the part-time karaoke host, and my good friend."

Dave came bounding up to them, Blaze his obvious goal. There was no mistaking things; he was flamboyantly gay. He was a robust man in a bright yellow T-shirt with a kitten riding a unicorn. A purple boa around his shoulders.

He pulled Blaze into a big bear hug and patted him on the back. "So, darling, what're we singing tonight? Or are you here just to watch?" Even his voice was fabulous.

Blaze's cheeks flush red. "Actually, I came to hear her sing." He nodded to her.

The pink on him was adorable, but when Dave's intrigued gaze landed on her, Grace's face was hot, too.

He grinned. "All right sweetheart, I get to pick your first song."

"That's sweet," she said. Her heart slid into overdrive. "But I have a song I always start with."

"Well, I guess my darling boy Blaze didn't tell you the rules of my karaoke club. I pick everyone's first song."

Great, I'm screwed.

CHAPTER 17

GRACE STOOD IN FRONT OF THE SCREEN WITH THE MICROPHONE IN her hand, wishing Hope had taken the offer to go first. Normally, she was all for kamikaze karaoke, but not this night. She had had nothing to drink yet and wanted to impress Blaze.

The flat screen TV in front of her lit up with bright lights and her name across the screen.

Dave left his booth and moved to stand next to Blaze, Hope, and Nick, his microphone still in hand.

With the first few notes of the song, she smiled. She didn't know the name of the song or the artist, but she remembered it from the radio; she'd sing along, as she did with most songs when she was driving.

Grace didn't know it well, but enough she wouldn't make too big of a fool of herself. She glanced over at the table.

Nick and Blaze appeared to be trying hard not to laugh as she sang.

She didn't know why; her singing wasn't that bad. She was a professional like them.

"Even though Solitude is my constant companion I
    know my salvation is there
I may be mental, I may even be oblivious
But love at first sight, I believe
How you keep this veil still confuses me Forever
    you are in my thoughts
Your past is irrelevant, move close to me Because
    we are meant to be"

WHEN SHE GOT to the chorus, Hope joined in; her bestie must've taken the microphone from Dave.

When the song was over, everybody cheered and Grace joined her friends at the table.

Blaze leaned over. "You do realize that was one of our songs, right? Dave was trying to be funny. But he doesn't know that you don't care who I am." His whisper shot a shiver down her spine and goosebumps broke out all over her arms.

"A *Razor's Edge* song? Really? I knew it from playing on the radio all the time."

Her cheeks flushed in embarrassment. Grace should've known it was one of their songs.

He kissed her cheek and smiled. No doubt, his way of telling her she was forgiven.

Hope was up next. She'd been lucky enough to get half of her drink down while Grace had been singing. Her friend took the microphone and got in place.

Grace giggled. Hope didn't know the song, but she knew it well. She'd always liked, *Raise Your Glass*, by Pink.

From the table, without a microphone, she sang along to give her friend direction in the song, taking a sip of her drink and raising the glass at the appropriate time.

After Hope was done, and returned to the table, Dave called out another name; it was neither Nick, nor Blaze.

"Nick, why aren't you singing?" Hope asked.

"I sing for a living," he said. "I just want to rest tonight."

"Are you freaking kidding me?" Grace jumped into their conversation. "I sing for a living, too, remember? Yet, I just did a song. Get your ass up there, and sing something."

Nick rolled his eyes, but nodded. "Yes, ma'am."

Blaze smiled big and touched her hand. "Another reason I adore you, you're not afraid to tell a pop star he's being an idiot."

"Sweetie, I know you guys are pop stars, but to me, you're not. It seems I know a few *Razor's Edge* songs but I don't know who *they* are. You're just Blaze and Nick."

He reached for her, slipping his hand through her hair to the nape of her neck so he could pull her closer for a deep kiss. He broke their kiss and let out a little sigh. "What're we gonna sing together, tonight babe?"

"WHAT ABOUT THIS ONE?" Blaze flipped through the book, pointing at a song.

"I don't know that one, sorry."

"This one?"

"Oh, God, no. I can't stand that song."

Grace was getting frustrated. Whenever they found a song one of them liked, the other didn't. The two rum and coke she'd had wasn't helping.

She came across one she'd first heard as a young girl. She had her fingers crossed and hoped and prayed Blaze knew it. She'd always wanted to sing it with someone, but knew no guys that could sing along.

"This one." Grace pointed to the title in the book.

He looked down, his eyes lingering for only a moment, before popping up he beamed.

"Does that mean you know this one?" she asked.

"Oh yeah, baby. I love this song." Blaze let Dave know what they had chosen.

Nick was also at the podium.

"Are you two singing, then?" Grace asked Hope.

"Yes."

A few more people got up and sang; some great, some made her wish she had earplugs. They all had a good time, and that was what mattered most.

After having two drinks, Grace needed the ladies room. She stepped in to the tiny room no bigger than a broom closet. She washed her hands, and she dared to glance in the mirror. Her cheeks were flushed red from the alcohol. Her vision was a little fuzzy. She stared into her own eyes, holding back tears that weren't there just a moment before. "What am I gonna do?" She said to the woman peering back at her. "I *need* to tell him why I can't be with him. But who am I really convincing? Hope's right. I need to let go. But do I let go of him, or my heart?" She shook her head back and forth, clearing away the remnants of her mini panic attack before putting her cold, damp hands over her cheeks to help with the redness.

She walked back to one of only six tables in the little bar, and the petite blonde barhop beckoned.

"Hey, sugar. I was asked to give you this."

She held up one... red... rose.

"What!"

"Some hottie caught my attention while I was out back having a smoke and he asked me to give it to you. He described you so well, I knew right who he was talkin' 'bout."

Ice dipped down her spine, causing the rum and coke to churn and threaten an eject.

"Did you get a good look at him? Can you tell me anything about him?"

"Sorry, honey. All I saw was a ball cap and a black jacket. I only gets about five minutes to have a cigarette, so I was in a hurry. It's pretty sweet, though."

'Sweet' was not the word she would use.

All those roses really were for me? Who sent them? How the hell do they know where I am?

She practically stumbled back to the table, sicker to her stomach with each step. Was someone watching her?

Thank God I leave in just a few hours. Maybe it's a fan of the play? It's over now. Go away.

No one said a word to her as she returned to her companions, making her feel like they hadn't noticed her moment at the bar.

Nick was called up and Grace noticed his song was one of *Journey's.*

"Oh! This is one of my favorite songs," Hope exclaimed, as he sang the intro to *Open Arms.* Grace sang along with him, because she knew all the words. She needed to think about something else, but kept obsessing.

Should I tell Blaze? What good would it do? I'm sure that was the end of it. There won't be any more.

Blaze bumped her with his shoulder, bringing her back to the moment. "Hey, not cool. You're supposed to be doing a duet with me, not Nick."

She shut her lips, which was hard to do because she liked the song. More importantly, had she spoken aloud? Grace shouldn't be trying to sing, and think, all while intoxicated. She pushed the rose, or roses, and its deliverer far from her mind. "Did Dave skip you? I thought you'd be next," she said when the next name was called and it wasn't Blaze.

"He didn't skip me. I told him I didn't want to go until I got to sing with you."

She leaned in and kissed him softly.

Two more drinks and a few bad karaokers later, Blaze and Grace were finally called up to do their duet together.

He offered her his hand to help her off her stool.

They went hand-in-hand and took their microphones from Dave. Their names lit up on the screen with the title of the song beneath it. *Close My Eyes Forever,* by Lita Ford and Ozzy Osborne.

It was such a sad and intense song, but Blaze's voice was so beautiful, it changed the way the song was interpreted.

I need to cool off. Damn, his voice does things to me! But I've only got these few hours left to spend with Hope.

Grace would see Blaze again soon, but she didn't know how long it would be before she saw her bestie again.

Nick and Hope were called up next. The song they chose was by Kid Rock and Sheryl Crow, called, *Picture.*

Nick ran his hands through his blond hair as he belted out the heartbreaking lyrics. He sounded like he was singing words true to him; his heart was fully in the performance.

Hope's voice held the same heartache.

Their voices blended together so perfectly, like they'd been singing as a couple for years. They looked like, it too. Such a beautiful sight. Even with her black heels on, giving her at least four extra inches, their foot height difference was obvious. Nick slid an arm over Hope bare shoulders as they finished singing and joined them back at the table.

Her friend's cheeks red from all the applause.

Grace kept begging Blaze to sing something on his own; she wanted to hear only *his* voice. He kept looking through the book but claimed he couldn't find the right song.

Before he ever got around to singing, Dave called out it was the final song; he was doing it as a crowd karaoke, everyone was to join in.

Grace laughed at the irony of the song; *Closing Time* by Semisonic.

The entire bar sang, the sound a joyous one.

Those who didn't know the verses had no problem catching on to the chorus.

They were still laughing as they walked back to the hotel,

arm-in-arm. When they walked into the lobby, Nick directed Hope to the elevator, hollering goodnight over his shoulder.

"Hope?" Grace called to her. "I won't get to see you in the morning."

Her friend slipped out from under Nick's arm, and headed back. "It was so good to see you! Thank you for everything! Call me tomorrow after you get settled, okay?"

They stepped back and peered at each other, their eyes swimming with tears. They always cried whenever they had to say goodbye.

This time, it was different. They weren't going back to their old lonely lives.

They had something completely new they were moving in to.

Grace hugged Hope one more time and watched as she joined Nick in the elevator.

Even though she was exhausted, she wanted nothing more than to make love to Blaze all night long.

As the door to the suite closed, their clothing hit the floor.

They both laughed when she tripped trying to get to the bed, her jeans around her ankles and her heels still on. She hit the floor and rolled on to her back, consumed with laughter.

Blaze offered a hand to help her up, but instead, she offered him her feet.

He took her heels and tossed them by the armchair, then grabbed the hem of her jeans and peeled them off the rest of the way.

Grace was left lying on the floor in only her underwear. She stared up at him. Was he going to take her on the floor? Blaze got down on his knees and straddled her legs. He leaned in so close, his hands on either side of her head.

She held her breath in anticipation of his kiss. She could feel the heat, yet he didn't touch her. It was driving her crazy. "Kiss me," Grace whispered into his lips.

"Not yet," he whispered back. "I want to drive you crazy."

She tittered. "Can we at least do it on the bed?"

"Not yet," he whispered again. Blaze moved his head, so she felt his breath in her ear, then down her neck.

Always so close, yet never touching.

Her body was coming alive; she was tingling all over, and he had yet to physically touch her.

His head dipped down to her right breast, millimeters away from her sensitive skin, causing her nipples to pucker as he teased her. He moved to the other one.

She closed her eyes, trying to block the heat of his breath. Grace's body exploded with a violent orgasm when he took her breast into the hot cavern of his mouth. She'd become sensitive and hyper-aware, and his assault sent her over the edge.

As he suckled, his hands snuck into her panties, her body still convulsing as he invaded her with his fingers.

She squirmed beneath him, needed all of him within her.

"Oh! Please... I can't take it anymore! I... need... Oh!" Her words fell on deaf ears.

Blaze obviously had his mind set to torture her, and nothing Grace said would change that.

He finally let go of her breast and slid her panties off.

She'd hoped that meant they'd move forward, but he had other things in mind.

They were now both completely naked and breathing hard.

Blaze continued to tease her until the wee hours of the morning.

Grace had never known a girl could orgasm so many times without actual penetration.

It wasn't until almost five in the morning when he finally entered her.

She was on her back, on the bed, and he brought her to a fevered pitch once again.

When she was about to explode again, Blaze moved so

quickly, plunging deep. Her body convulsed as he possessed her, a graceful dance of flesh.

"Blaze! I'm... I'm gonna..." She couldn't form a full sentence. Her breathing was labored, and another wave built.

Blaze drove into her, harder and faster, trying to join her in another explosion.

They both cried out as they climaxed together.

CHAPTER 18

GRACE WAS EXHAUSTED. SHE HAD A FLIGHT IN LESS THAN FOUR hours and needed to get to at least an hour of sleep. If she didn't take the opportunity, it would never happen.

That wouldn't be good for either of them.

In the bed, about to drift off, her head rested on his chest, his arm over her shoulder, holding her close to him.

It's now or never.

"Blaze?"

"Hmm?" He too, was barely conscious.

"I need to tell you something. Explain something."

"What, babe?"

She could feel the vibrations of his voice through his chest. "Why I can't do this."

He shifted beneath her, causing her to move and sit up. "Do what?" Now Blaze was full of concern.

Tears pricked in the back of her eyes. Grace squeezed them shut, trying to stop herself from letting them fall. She slipped off the bed, grabbed the robe from the bathroom and paced.

"Grace? What is going on?" He started to get up but she held up a hand to stop him.

"I mentioned last night, my parents are deceased?"

He nodded, pulling one knee up toward his chest.

"My father died quite a few years ago serving in the Middle East." The rush of memories made her wipe at the tears that rolled down her cheek. She and her mother had been in the kitchen baking brownies for her high school theater's annual bake sale, when there was a knock on the door.

"I remember Mom being covered in cocoa powder, because we'd just gotten into a little food fight. She opened the door with one of her usual huge smiles on her face. As I watched from the kitchen, that look faded into a grimace and there was only fear and desperation when she saw the two men standing there, and what they represented."

An Army Casualty Notification Officer and Chaplin in their dress uniforms, remorseful and haggard, at the front door with the heartbreaking news.

"My mother was never the same after that. She and Dad had the love every girl dreams of, and what fairy tales are written about. Without Dad, she suffered from depression, and became a shell of her former self. She loved my father with all her heart and soul. When he died, she died, just more slowly. I woke up one morning a few months later, to find Mom had taken her own life, she just couldn't live without him. I was only nineteen." Grace stopped pacing when she felt his arms wrap tightly around her. She hadn't heard him leave the bed.

Blaze just held her and she tried her best to keep from sobbing. She hadn't shared this with *anyone*. Not even Hope knew this much. "I'm all alone," she whispered.

"Oh, baby. You don't have to be. I'm here." He kissed the top of her head, causing the dam of tears to come flowing.

Grace pushed away from him, needing to get far away.

"Grace?"

"That's why I can't do this! I can't be like my mother. I *need* to be alone."

He reached for her again, but she ran to the bathroom, closing the door and pressing her head against it, trying hard to stop crying.

"Come out, baby," he said from the other side.

"I can't."

"Yes, you can. Come out here and tell me why you're so scared."

Her breath came in rasps, making her light headed. She pushed herself off the door and straightened. She turned to the woman in the mirror, put her hands on the counter, leaning in close to the reflection.

Why are you so afraid? Because I think I—

"Baby?"

She heard the jiggle of the handle seconds before the door opened.

Blaze stepped in, his eyes dark pools of torment. "What is this really about?" He gripped the door jam, blocking any chance of her escape.

"I'm afraid, all right!" Grace yelled. Her cheeks flushed hot with embarrassment. She hadn't meant to take it out on him.

His face softened, so did his hold on the door frame. His white knuckles flooded with color as he brought his hands down to offer her his open arms.

She hesitated.

"It's okay, babe. Let's figure this out together."

She was hurting him just as much as herself.

Grace had meant to have a talk with him, not a dramatic scene worthy of the stage. She stepped into his embrace and let him hold her, She buried her face in his chest.

At least I don't have to look in to those beautiful eyes of his, when I tell him goodbye.

"Now, Grace. Talk to me."

She sighed.

"After my heart was broken, it took a while for me to understand even though the pain was intense, wasn't real love. True love destroyed my mother. And a simple heartbreak damaged me." Grace sniffled. "If I could hurt that bad from losing my friend, what would happen, if I found real love and lost it. The women in my family love too deeply. So I swore I'd never put myself in a situation where I could get hurt again. If I have no relationships, I don't have to keep my guard up."

Blaze took a deep breath, slowly releasing it before speaking. "You don't have to be madly in love to have a relationship. You and Hope have a relationship. You're best friends. Are you afraid of that?"

"No, but that's different."

"Is it?" His voice reverberated through his chest. "If something happened to her, and she died, you'd be devastated, crushed. But you'd still go on, wouldn't you? You're a strong woman, Grace. You should give yourself more credit, okay?"

"All right," was all she could muster.

"Don't walk away from us, when we're just getting started. Let's try and get a little sleep. You have a long day ahead."

Grace didn't argue with him. She was spent, and he was right.

She crawled into bed and curled up beside him.

SHE HADN'T WANTED to say goodbye.

Grace had tried so hard to be quiet and just leave.

She'd intended to write him a note.

She sat at the desk and grabbed the hotel notepad and pen when the chair had let out a horrendous creak.

Blaze had sat upright, rubbing his eyes like a little boy. "What're you doing?"

"Leaving a note before the taxi gets me," she whispered.

"I don't think so. I'll take you. It's the right thing to do; I need to. Don't deny me that little pleasure."

"Blaze, that's kind, but I'm worried my luggage won't fit in the trunk."

"Sweetie, I'm a pro. I got this."

They left the hotel just as the sun was rising.

It was so beautiful to watch as he drove them in silence.

She was grateful he didn't bring up their last hours together, but fearful because it was like it hadn't happened. "Just drop me off at departures."

Wishful thinking.

"Grace, this too, is a battle you will not win."

They parked in the garage and Blaze walked her to her airline check-in then to the security area.

They had to say goodbye.

His kiss said everything.

There was no need for words.

Maybe he is worth dying for...

GRACE TOOK a deep breath as she stepped out to gaze upon the Denver sky.

The air is so different here than anywhere else. I will miss this.

With her luggage trolley and her purse over her shoulder, she sought a taxi.

She sat in the back of the odd smelling yellow car, Blaze consumed her thoughts.

How can I feel like this? What if I wasn't moving to L.A., what if Blaze hadn't been at the masquerade... stop!

She'd drive herself crazy obsessing like that.

Grace forced herself to lay her head back and close her eyes until she got to her apartment, but she couldn't stop thinking about that morning with Blaze.

As happy as I am to see home, I'm not looking forward to the next steps.

She'd probably pull a muscle or have a heart attack since she had to carry every piece of her luggage up the four flights of stairs. The stupid elevator was still broken. She'd lived in the apartment almost nine years; after both her parents had died. In all those years, the elevator had worked less than half of the time. That was why the building has such a high turnover rate

Grace didn't know her neighbors, if she even had any, but it didn't matter now, she was leaving. Too bad, she could use help packing. On the plus side, she could turn her music up loud and dance around her place as she did her chores and she had no one to complain about it.

When she got to her door, there was a long white box propped up against the door. Management knew she was supposed to be gone for months, and she hadn't been due back for another week.

So why the hell is there anything in front of my door?

She let her bags slide off her shoulder and onto the floor so she could unlock the door. The box fell into the room as the door opened. She didn't grab it, and left her bags as she reached for the light.

Home sweet home. Everything looks the same.

She'd probably have an inch of dust on her antique dining table. The red curtains were still closed, giving the room a dark, mysterious feel to it, even though it was midday. Grace pulled them opened, dust mites flying in the sudden burst of sunshine. She had to squint her eyes to adjust.

When she got everything inside she concentrated on the package.

She frowned.

A dozen roses, but they were dead.

A cold chill went down her spine. This was worse than the single random roses.

Who is sending these! How long they been sitting out there?

She picked up a small white card that'd fallen down by the stems. She flipped it over to read it.

One rose for each week we performed. A reminder
of all the times we kissed. If I can get you to love
roses, I can get you to love me.
—Charles.

"What the hell?" Grace said aloud. There was no way her costar could've known she'd be back already, and the flowers had been dead for a while.

What had Charles been thinking? She didn't like roses, and he knew it.

When Grace was little, she'd had a horrible experience, where the aroma of roses had filled her senses.

She'd been so afraid.

She'd told Charles the story, and he knew how afraid she'd been that night.

Why would he send roses? Had the others been from him, too?

Grace narrowed her eyes, then swept her gaze throughout her place. She sighed, and closed the lid to the box. She had a million and twelve things to do, all before her boxes arrived at three that afternoon.

CHAPTER 19

"GOOD AFTERNOON, JEANETTE. CAN I GET MY MAIL?" GRACE HAD
been gone for months, so it was likely a great deal.

"You're back early," the office manager said as she pulled a
large box from under the counter.

"Yeah, got a promotion with the theater. Didn't you get my
email, about moving out?"

"Oh, sweetie, this old building has more issues than *TV Guide*.
I haven't had internet in over two weeks. You're the last one
living on that floor. I think Allen is gonna start the renovations as
soon as you move out. Thank God. You get settled and we'll chat
in a few days."

"Thanks. I appreciate it. This one box alone will keep me
busy, not to mention packing!"

More than half the container would be junk mail, but she still
had to go through it all. She didn't want to pack tons of mail to
move to L.A., she already had enough on her plate when she got
back.

Grace sat on the floor and dumped the entire box in front of
her so she could sort her mail, a waiting garbage bag beside her.

One pile was important stuff, one was fun to read things, and the rest was for the trash.

Halfway into the mess, she found two envelopes from Charles.

"This makes no sense, we'd been together doing the show, so why would he send this though the mail?"

She slid open the top of the letter with the oldest postmark date. It was from two weeks ago.

My dearest Grace,

For weeks now I've been trying to find the words to tell you how I feel. I've written and performed songs before, so why do I find this so difficult to do? I know you won't read this until after our production is done, but I had to get it out of me now before I went insane.

The first moment I saw you, I knew I would fall in love with you. There's just something about you that draws everyone in. I don't know if it's your smile or your laugh, or just who you are, but you owned my heart from our first introduction, when you tripped and fell into my arms.

I hope our age difference doesn't keep us apart. Just like being on stage no one would know that you're eight years older than me.

I know you told me when we started this production, no relationships until it's over. We are almost there and it is killing me to wait. I hope by the time you read this I've gotten the courage enough to tell you, my feelings haven't changed, and this is all redundant.

But no matter what, just know I'm in love with you,
  and I always will be.

Yours forever, Charles

GRACE SET the letter down on the floor and stared. He'd confronted her last week. She hadn't been convinced he loved her, and now this?

Why didn't I see this?

She was afraid to open the next letter. It was postmarked a week ago.

My dearest Grace,

I've decided I'm going to tell you, I can't take it
  anymore, I'm going crazy over this. Every once
  in a while I find myself suffering from jealousy.
I know you have an infectious laugh and smile but I
  can't stand anymore to see all of the guys
  begging for your attention, and you don't even
  see it.
Does it mean you don't see my feelings for you? I
  hate having to share your attention with
  everyone else. What I wouldn't give to have that
  smile be just for me.
Someday, it will be. I just know it. Soon enough
  you'll know how I feel.
I love you, Grace.

Yours forever, Charles.

A KNOT FORMED in the middle of her chest and hardened as it grew, until pain throbbed around it.

"Oh, Charles."

The letter seemed harmless. A sweet declaration, but was there more?

Whispers in the back of her mind made her focus keen on reading through the lines. Did she have something to worry about?

He'd attacked Blaze, after all.

She rummaged through what was left on the floor, desperate to see if there was anything else from him.

A sigh floated from her lips when there was nothing more. "Thank God."

Grace picked up the two letters and tucked them away, inside the box of dead roses. She left it sitting at the table as she went back to her mail organizing.

Her boxes had arrived and she was working to get as much packed up as she could, as fast as she could.

Blaze had promised he'd call after his rehearsals, so she was expecting to hear from him anytime. When the phone rang, it was unfortunately short and sweet.

"Hey, babe, I miss you."

Just hearing his voice filled her with so much emotion.

She'd told him of her past, her fear of loving someone, and it hadn't scared him away. Even though they were just starting out, he wouldn't let her give up.

He made her want to live.

Grace could feel her guard going up. It made her think of the flowers. Worry threatened to take her over.

"I made it back to my apartment and got my mail but I should tell—"

"BJ!" someone in the background yelled. "Just because we're finished with rehearsing, doesn't mean we're done with you!"

"I gotta go, babe, but I'll call you, later."

He was gone before she could even say goodbye.

Grace sighed; her apartment would keep her busy.

Over the next few hours, she got much of her kitchen packed up, leaving only a few things she'd need to use until she left.

She'd gone through her apartment and made a list of the things that couldn't get packed until the last moment, like towels and washcloths, and other important essentials.

Grace turned her tunes up to a nonintrusive level, and danced around while she put things in boxes.

If she wanted to take an hour off tomorrow, to watch Blaze and his group perform live on the *Ellen* show, she needed to keep her ass in gear.

She ordered dinner from her favorite Chinese restaurant and busted open a bottle of wine she had been holding on to, saving for a special occasion. "I can't think it anything more special than the adventure I'm about to embark on."

If she only had one glass a night, she could enjoy the bottle every night before she left.

Finishing the wine would be like finishing her life in Denver.

Bittersweet.

Fatigue from the day caught up with her, and Grace crawled into bed. She rolled under her covers, her stuffed tiger in her arms and reached for her phone to make a call. She wanted to hear Blaze's voice before she went to sleep.

She hadn't realized how much she'd missed her own bed until she was lying curled up with her favorite comforter.

She missed Blaze more.

That scared her.

He made her ready to live, to try. To be willing to give her heart away. It had been just her for so long, but now as she lay in bed alone, she felt… incomplete.

"Just a more days babe, a few more days and I'll see you again."

She smiled as comfort from his words washed over her.

Grace could survive a few more days.

"Actually, I get to see you tomorrow! Or would that be today, since it's after midnight?"

"Tomorrow, it's only 11:47 here. But that's just on TV, it's not the same."

"I know." She let out a tired sigh. "Can't believe how much I miss you, and Hope; even Nick, too."

"Speaking of Hope, did she tell you she's coming to watch the show tomorrow? Nick's gonna bring her backstage. I'm sure she'll call you tomorrow night and tell you all about it."

Grace let out a tired sigh. "I wish I could be there to cheer on. I want to support you."

"No worries, baby, you're doing what you need to do. And soon I'll see you every day, so it won't matter anymore."

Her answer was taken by a huge yawn.

"Grace, go to sleep. I'll talk to you tomorrow, okay, baby?"

"Okay," she managed to say through another big yawn.

♪♫

GRACE HAD LOST track of how many times she'd moved as a child, and packing was just another part of life. In all those years, she'd never been nearly as motivated to pack as quickly as she was to leave Denver.

She had to be on the road by Saturday morning at the latest, but her goal was to be out by Friday. The sooner she could have everything in boxes, the sooner she'd be back with Blaze.

"Blaze." She said his name again and let it roll over her tongue.

If anyone had asked her, even a week before, where she thought her life would be, it definitely wouldn't have been where it was headed.

She'd sworn never to love, or even put herself in a position where love could grow. There she was, having her heart stolen by a man who'd broken a million.

I'm absolutely terrified, and really excited. What the hell?

Grace was looking forward to each and every day ahead of her, ready to leave her past and her fear behind her.

Her dream had come true, she'd become a successful actor, and now would be a permanent part of a theater company. Most importantly, a dream she thought she never wanted, had been presented to her and she'd hesitantly accepted it.

Blaze.

> I know you are busy with rehearsals and getting
> ready for the show, but I just wanted to let you
> know I'm thinking of you

She sent him the text message and put her TV on NBC, the channel the *Ellen* show would be on. She'd never miss it.

The rest of her time flew by; she was just that motivated. Just before three, she stood in the center of her living room and scanned the mountains of boxes. If she could pick up the trailer sooner, she could leave in the morning. Maybe she could check on it?

After the show?

Grace dashed to the kitchen and grabbed a bag of potato chips and French onion dip, with a Mountain Dew from the fridge and sat on her half buried couch, ready for the show to start.

The show began, and the audience—no doubt crazed girls— were already screaming.

"I'm Ellen. But you already knew that. I can't wait to tell you about my guests for the day. The awesome band, Razor's Edge. *Once a year I do a live show so people can see how hard it really is hosting a talk show. There's no delay, no pausing the show, so even though I do my best to prepare my guests so they wouldn't screw anything up, something always happens."*

She asked the guys to come on stage and introduced them one by one. They looked so dapper in their matching outfits. All five of them wore black and rust. On each guy, the piece they wore was different; Blaze had on rust-colored pants, but Nick had on a rust-colored jacket.

"So, what have each of you been up to lately?" Ellen prompted. *"We'll start with Thomas."*

The audience screamed.

"What have I been up to? About 5' 8. I think I'm shrinking." He smiled and sobered after the crowd's laughter. *"We've been working on the newest album, that should come out just after Christmas."*

"Dwaine, here. I, uh... I'm about to become a daddy, again."

"Hi. I'm Scott," member number three said, in a voice so rich and smooth. *"I'm just glad to be rejoining my brothers from another mother. I needed some time to reflect. But here I am."*

Ellen turned to Blaze next.

"What have I been up to lately? Well, I fell in love."

Grace's heart cantered, all the girls on the TV screamed even louder.

Instead of looking at Ellen, Blaze faced the camera nearest him. *"Hey baby, I know you're watching.*

"I miss you, and I just want you to know, I'll never break your heart. I love you."

Grace melted into the couch.

What the fuck!

Hadn't she just told him her fear of loving someone?

What did she truly feel? She didn't expect to discover that for a long time. She needed time.

How can he love me?

Her moment ended when Nick smacked her man with the back of his hand across his chest. Her irritation melted away and she fell into giggles.

"Dude, not cool. I was going to talk about how I fell in love."

Ellen, the comedian she was, jumped right in. *"And your fans are okay with the two of you falling in love with each other?"*

Nick stuttered and turned bright red. He pointed off camera.

"A girl a girl, I promise! I fell in love with a girl. She's standing right over there."

The camera whirled to reveal Hope standing with band management. She was as bright crimson as Nick had been. No doubt she was embarrassed.

Grace beamed; half-jealous and half-relieved she wasn't there.

"Well, then. I think it's time to hear if these boys still have it going on. So, what are you going to sing?"

"We're gonna treat ya'll to something from our new album, a song called Peach," Scott announced.

Grace watched in absolute awe as they performed and danced together. They were a perfect team, brothers from another mother as they called themselves. There was no doubt they had millions of fans. They were beyond amazing.

One of them was hers.

She was so wrapped up in watching, she almost missed the continuous knock at her door. She glanced at the clock on her cable box. It was just a little after three. Richard was supposed to send her keys. No doubt it was them.

She hated to miss any of the performance but she had to answer the door. Grace threw open the door, intending to grab and dash.

She never got the chance.

Something was shoved in her face, and an odd smell overtook her senses; burned her lungs.

Then the world went black.

CHAPTER 20

GRACE WAS AFRAID TO OPEN HER EYES; SHE WAS AFRAID OF WHAT was before her. One of her silk scarves was wrapped around her mouth and panic snaked around her spine and inched up, constricting.

She couldn't cry out.

Using senses other than sight, she tried to assess what was going on. She was in one of her antique dining room chairs, the head chair that had the armrests. Her legs were bound to the legs of the chair with packing tape, and so were her hands to the armrest.

The TV was still on, and she could hear Blaze's voice in the background.

She listened to the deep sound of his voice, letting it resonate through her and bring her comfort. The words didn't matter. Just his tone helped.

Grace took a deep breath through her nose and instantly regretted it.

He was close, so close she could smell him.

His cologne was musky and it mixed with his own personal smell so well.

It had once been an aroma to bring her comfort, and now it was filled her with dread.

How could my dearest friend do something as horrendous as this?

"Open your eyes, Grace."

His voice was still beautiful and familiar, but now sounded ominous.

"Open your eyes, Grace. I know you're awake."

Her stomach churned with unease and dread. But she still refused to do as he asked.

"Damn it, Grace, why can't you look at me?"

She opened her eyes and glared.

Charles took a step back.

She noticed the green around his eyes and the splint on his nose from where Blaze had broken it. It made him look even more deranged.

I really hope that hurt.

He took a step closer to her and ran the back of his knuckles down her cheek.

She recoiled from his touch.

Rage dominated his expression. His cheeks were flushed red and there were beads of sweat on his forehead. He grabbed her cheeks then, squeezing hard, causing her mouth into the shape of an 'O' behind the scarf.

Grace tried pulling her head out of his grasp, but his grip was too strong.

"I wouldn't do that, Grace." His voice was sickly sweet.

Although her mouth was full of her silk scarf, she still bitched him out, but her words didn't come through clear.

His eyes hardened even more; so maybe she'd been successful, after all.

Before he had a chance to respond with his newfound anger, there was a knock at the door.

Thank God, it has to be the FedEx guy.

The knocking continued, despite no answer.

Charles growled and narrowed his already beady eyes, then stalked to the door, putting his finger over his lips to tell her to be quiet.

Yeah. Right.

If she could manage to get attention, she was going to do it.

Grace started rocking her chair back and forth, trying to make as much noise as possible. She screamed as hard as she could, which wasn't very loud with the fabric shoved in her mouth.

The knocking stopped.

Dammit.

She glanced back to the television screen; the five men were still singing and dancing.

If she didn't answer her phone for the next few days; if she didn't show up in L.A. soon, would they come looking for her?

Will I still be alive?

Charles noticed she was watching the television, and must've realized what was on the screen. He grabbed the remote off the coffee table and turned off the tv.

Her heart broke just a little bit as he took her comfort away.

He prowled back to her and raised his hand, remote still clutched in his fingers.

He wouldn't—

Agony exploded in her face and took over her senses. The hard plastic only added to the impact. Her vision blurred. Something warm trickled down the side of her head.

"He can't have you! You. Are. Mine, Grace! You have been since the day we met."

Her head spun, and she struggled to focus.

His face was in triplicate, but she locked onto his eyes.

They were all brown now, not a hint of the beautiful golden ring he used to have.

Charles rushed back to her, gripping her cheeks again, but this time gently.

Grace still winced and tried to move from his hold.

"Oh, Grace! I'm so sorry!" He ran to the kitchen and rummaged through the empty drawers.

"Damn it! Where are your towels?"

She glared.

I can't answer; you gagged me, asshole.

He grabbed paper towels from the counter and she heard the faucet turn on and off.

Charles dabbed at her temple with the semi-wet paper towel, apologizing over and over, that he hadn't meant to hit her. "This is all BJ's fault. If that bastard hadn't..."

Blaze. He means Blaze.

"I really am sorry, Grace."

The pain in her head hadn't dissipated. If anything, her headache had gotten worse from listening to his apologies.

After he had cleaned her all up, and the bleeding had stopped, Charles leaned down and kissed her temple, then her cheek.

Goosebumps erupt all over her form. It wasn't pleasure, like when Blaze kissed her, but more like repulsion. Her body prickled and she squirmed on the chair, she couldn't help it. Once again she tried to pull away, but it angered him.

Charles grabbed a handful of her hair and yanked her head back, exposing her throat.

Grace froze and swallowed. Twice. She ordered herself not to move, but ice froze her blood and she didn't think she could anyway. She shut her eyes. She felt his hot breath against her neck.

He trailed kisses across her throat, down toward her collarbone.

Tears stung her eyes, and she crushed them even tighter. Couldn't let him see her cry. Grace tensed, going tight all over.

Charles must've felt it, too.

He let go of her hair and moved away.

She kept her eyes sealed shut, just listening to assess.

He sighed, picked up her keys. "I'll be right back, Grace, don't move." Then the door to her apartment opened.

She let out a deep breath when the key turned in the lock. She wrenched her hands, trying to break the tape.

All she did was rub all the hair off her wrists. Grace had seen enough scary movies to know that knocking the chair over did no good.

This chair was as solid as they could get.

There was no hope of it breaking.

She glanced at the time on the cable box. It was after four now.

Blaze would call soon.

Please! Let him call before Charles returns.

Not that it would do her any good. Her cellphone was on the table in front of the couch. She'd never be able to reach it.

If I don't answer, will he keep calling?

The silk scarf was drying her mouth, and the salty chips she'd eaten before Charles had arrived, didn't help either.

Grace tried to push the fabric out of her mouth with her tongue, to no avail. She put her head on her left shoulder, pressed her cheek down, and did her best to work the scarf out of her mouth. It still wouldn't be moved.

He'd tied it too well, and too tight.

Just as her tears of frustration fell, her cell rang. Even from her seat, she could see the name on the Caller ID.

Blaze.

A short time later, the alert for voicemail chimed.

Please, call again, and keep calling.

She prayed it didn't take him days to come look for her.

THE ROOM WAS COMPLETELY DARK, aside from the faint glow of

the clock on her cable box. Grace glanced at it; it was already after ten p.m.

Charles had been gone for over five hours. He hadn't turned on the lights before he'd left.

It was just as well, she'd been crying the whole time. Her eyes felt puffy; they were likely red. When he came back and lit her place up, he'd see everything.

She heard the key turn in the lock.

He was back.

She didn't want Charles to know she'd been crying. Grace did her best to quickly wipe her tears off on her shoulders. She was never one to cry, but couldn't stop the tears from falling each time Blaze had continued to call. She would've liked to say they were tears of hope, but eventually, they'd turned into drops of fear.

Will he come looking for me when I don't answer the phone after the one-hundredth time?

"Grace, I'm back." His voice almost sounded cheerful, as if they were back to their everyday friendship.

Had he forgotten he'd kidnapped her in her own home?

Grace gritted her teeth. Her fear dissolved, and once again was replaced with anger.

The door closed and in the same instant, Charles turned on the lights.

She blinked a few times, letting her vision adjust the brightness. She glared at Charles, and the first thing she noticed was his bloodshot eyes. Had he been crying?

Is he feeling remorseful for what he's done?

It wasn't until he moved a little closer and she smelled it. He hadn't been crying; he was high.

His movements were sluggish and he almost tripped.

Once again he ran his knuckle down the side of her face.

This time Grace didn't pull away. She tried to focus on something else, to get the feeling of his touch out of her mind. So she concentrated on her throat. It was raw from a mixture of dehydration and trying to scream with a scarf blocking the sound. She needed water, but couldn't even ask.

Charles's time away had given her time to think. Grace had learned one lesson; don't make him angry.

He'd told her he used to have a short temper, but he'd learned to control it with meditation.

Her former costar had proven today that wasn't true.

When he'd hit her, it was because she'd been looking at Blaze on the TV. Charles had said more than once she was meant to be his.

I'm gonna have to turn this into a game. I have to make him think I love him.

It might be the only she'd get free.

Grace reached deep inside and looked at him with not a glare, but all the pleading she could manage, hoping he could see it in her eyes. She tried to look down at her mouth, then back at him.

He didn't seem to understand, his expression was confused.

Please remove the scarf. She tried to push her thought into his brain.

Charles quirked his head to the side again, obviously still confused.

She said the same thing over and over, but the sound wouldn't breach the barrier even when she tried to shout.

"Gracie, I can't understand you."

She nodded quickly. She couldn't gesture, since her hands were still bound.

Charles moved to stand behind her. "Be still, let me untie this. But promise not to scream."

All I want to do is scream.

Her throat was sore and raw. She doubted she'd be able to make a substantial sound.

Grace also didn't want to incur his wrath, as there was no way she could defend herself; still taped to the chair.

Besides, this is a game, and I'm about to change the rules.

If she was compliant and made him think she loved him, maybe he'd cut the tape and let her out of the chair.

She hadn't realized how tight the scarf was until he removed it. Pain throbbed from the corners of her mouth. The skin was split, like the worst chapped lips and without the pressure, discomfort was making it worse.

Blood had dried to the fabric and when Charles pulled it away, the scabbing went, too.

Her tongue went to the left side of her mouth and she hissed in at the burning sensation.

She inhaled and Charles's glare said he thought she would scream. Grace wished she could have. It wouldn't have done any good. She had no neighbors.

He quickly covered her mouth before she even had a chance to exhale. "I said no screaming, Grace. Do I need to stuff that back in your mouth?"

She shook her head and he inched his hand back, but kept it close.

"I was just taking a breath. That's all. I wouldn't scream, you asked me not to." The words came out deep and raspy, sounding like a chain-smoking old woman.

He sighed and moved his hand the rest of the way back.

Grace needed to take her first step toward getting free.

She needed him to start trusting her.

"Charles," she whispered, trying to save her voice. "Can I please get some water? I'm so thirsty." She was hoping he'd remove the tape from one of her hands so she could hold a cup.

She wasn't so lucky.

Charles went to the kitchen without answering and rummaged through what little was left in the cupboards and drawers.

She closed her eyes, waiting for him to return.

When he came back, she wasn't sure if she should laugh

or cry.

"Here, baby. Take a sip." His voice was sweet as honey but grated on her spine.

Grace opened her eyes.

Charles was standing with a Styrofoam cup full of water, with a straw sticking out.

Damn it! Why didn't I pack the straws?

She always had straws because of her super sensitive teeth. She used every time she had ice in a cup. She'd left them in the cupboard along with paper plates.

She wouldn't be getting her hands free, after all. Grace sighed and leaned forward so she could get a drink.

She needed to get out of the chair. Without taking another breath, she downed the water. The slurping sound of an empty cup filled the otherwise silent room. "Please, Charles. Can I have another glass?" The liquid soothed her throat a little.

Grace didn't want him to know her voice was stronger, so she spoke with as much forced raspy-ness as she could, without hurting her vocal cords more.

Four cups of water later, she needed to wait a little while. Nature would hit and he would have to let her up. Or so she hoped.

In the meantime, Charles paced the room. He didn't speak, just wore a path in the carpet.

"Charles?" Grace whispered.

He paused, pinning her with his gaze.

"I need to go to the bathroom." She left it at that.

He ran his hands through his blond hair, causing it to stick up. Charles was like a little boy trying to figure out a difficult puzzle. His eyes seemed out of focus before he glanced down the hallway that led to her bathroom. Slowly, he faced her again. He blinked a few times before his eyes landed on her face again. He just nodded.

Her heart raced. Grace did need to relieve herself, and was

prepared to make a mess if he didn't release her.

Charles went to the kitchen and picked up a pair of scissors she had in the knife block. "I'm sorry, Grace. It has to be this way." He stepped up to the chair. "I will release your feet, and with your hands still on the chair, we are gonna walk to the bathroom."

Seriously, is he crazy? I'm going to carry this heavy chair? To the bathroom?

He carefully cut away at the tape.

Grace was grateful she'd shaved the night before. Otherwise, it would've been far more painful when he peeled the remaining tape off her poor skin.

Charles set the scissors down, and grabbed the back of the chair. He took most of the weight off her wrists as they walked toward her bathroom.

It took minutes to get there. Grace had to have him stop every few feet.

It was painful to have to walk hunched over with her wrists taped to the chair. If she'd had any arm hair left, it was surely gone by now.

They stood just outside the bathroom door and he set the chair down, her backside joining it again.

Then, without a word, he walked away.

Grace tried to look over her shoulder to see where he was going, but couldn't stretch that far. She could hear him in the other room.

Charles returned with something in his hands. He set it down on top of her dresser beside the bathroom door. "I'm sorry, Grace. But it has to be done my way."

He lifted something and brought to her face.

She tried not to breathe. She fought, shaking her head, not willing to let him knock her out again.

It was a fight she couldn't win.

Her chest burned with the lack of oxygen.

CHAPTER 21

"Oh, my sweet, Gracie," Charles crooned as he shampooed her tresses. "Your hair's soft like silk. I hated that you had to hide it when we were on stage. You shouldn't have. It's so beautiful. Far superior to the drab brown curly wig they made you wear." They sat in the bathtub, and he held her unconscious body upright against his chest with one arm. He used the other to wash her. "I've waited so long for this, so long to hold you in my arms so I can take care of you, love you. It's so worth the wait." He took great care as he cleansed her body.

Grace had lost all control of her functions when he'd used the chloroform. He'd known it might happen, but had been wiling to take the chance.

"We couldn't have you get dehydrated. It's bad for the vocal cords," he continued to chat with her unresponsive form. "I need us to sing together again. Our voices were made to be together, just like us." He conditioned her hair as well, working the cream thoroughly to every strand.

Charles rinsed her hair, using a bowl he had found in the kitchen. He continued to sit in the tub until the water drained out. Then carefully laid her head down in the base of the tub, as he stood, grabbed the towel hanging over the shower rod.

He quickly dried himself off before turning back to the tub. "Come, my love."

It took a lot more strength to get her out of the tub than it had been to get her in. The muscles in his biceps burned when he moved her to the rug on the bathroom floor. He toweled her dry. "We need a bigger apartment." He slipped his arms under her, locking his fingers together just under her breasts.

He dragged her into the bedroom, the heels of her feet leaving a trail in the carpet. "This is too small. Maybe in Florida?"

Charles tugged the comforter down the bed, and hefted Grace to the side to the bed closest to the door. The left side.

He arranged her so her hands were behind her again. He got the tape and secured her. "It's not time yet. You're not ready yet. Soon, my love." He pulled the thick blanket over her nudity and returned to the bathroom to clean the mess.

Charles glanced at the clock on the nightstand and he crawled in to bed beside her. It was almost midnight. He didn't want to have anyone or anything tell him what to do, so he yanked the cord out of the wall, forcing time to disappear from his sight.

He laid back, only to get an uncomfortable jab in the back. He reached behind him and found a tacky pink and orange tiger. He spiked it to the floor with distain. "She won't need you anymore. She has *me* to keep her company in her bed now." He settled in, pulling the comforter over his bare skin. Charles closed his eyes; taking in the scent of her into his lungs, her name on his lips.

GRACE'S EYES opened only to find darkness. She was on her bed, her comforter wrapped close to her. She was also curled up on her right side, facing into the bed.

She almost always slept either on her left side or on her stomach. She knew where she was, but something didn't seem right. Maybe she'd just had a horrible dream?

She startled.

Grace couldn't move her hands; they were bound behind her back. She took in a deep breath, trying to steady herself.

In that one moment of air, she recognized the scent of her body wash and shampoo, and Charles's cologne. Her heart thumped hard. Everything came crashing into her.

She wasn't alone in her bed.

The last thing she could recall was heading to the bathroom, still strapped to the chair. There was no memory of taking a shower, yet there was no denying she'd taken one. Her hair was wet, too.

Her throat was raw, as if she'd been drinking liquid fire.

Grace's eyes had adjusted to the darkness and Charles's face was only inches from hers.

He was asleep and looked so peaceful, child-like.

She couldn't fathom how someone so sweet, someone who'd been a dear friend to her could do something like this.

Her eyes traveled over his features, and down to his throat.

He didn't have a shirt on.

She took stock of her own clothing—or lack thereof.

It should've been the first thing she'd noticed.

Grace *never* slept in the nude.

As if her heart could pound any harder, she tried to determine if there was anything else off with her body.

Did he...hurt...me while I was unconscious?

She felt...normal.

Grace let out the breath she'd been holding.

When she'd made love to Blaze, her body had felt deliciously sore the next morning.

If Charles had done something to me, I'd know, wouldn't I?

The tears fell, unchecked, so she turned her face into the pillow and sobbed.

. . .

SUNLIGHT SPILLED across her face and Grace blinked the sleep from her eyes. Her shoulders were cramped and all she wanted to do was stretch, but she couldn't. She dared to glance to the other side of the bed. Relief washed over her when she found it empty.

His scent still lingered.

Grace yawned. She wasn't gagged.

Still wouldn't do her any good to scream. She didn't have enough neighbors for anyone hear her, and she could hear Charles moving around in her kitchen.

Besides, her throat was so raw. Whatever he'd stuffed in her face to make her pass out had horrible lingering effects. She felt like she had a wicked hangover.

Grace lay in the bed, as silent as she could be, listening to him move about.

He was singing to himself. It sounded like he a song from their play.

She strained her ears.

He must've left the kitchen, because she could hear him clearer.

The song had shifted. He was now singing, *"It Was True."*

Was that good or bad?

"Once the sky was new,
Once the spring had come
Once the scene was set for a night of fun. The stars
    adorned the night
Then clarity was sung:
It was true.
It was true.
It was true."

As the song went on, he was moving into the bedroom.

She pretended to be asleep.

Charles stopped singing.

The next part of the song was supposed to be hers.

"Gracie. I know you're awake." His voice was just above a whisper. "Gracie? Sing for me. Please? Sing your part."

Grace slowly opened her eyes.

He stood to the side of her bed. His shirt was back on, but his nose splint was missing. He looked at her with such love in his eyes.

It wasn't love.

She just wanted to cry.

If you love someone, you don't tie them up.

She shook her head.

"Gracie? Why won't you sing with me? The first time we sang this song, at auditions, I knew then I loved you. Sing with me."

She tried to speak, simply to tell him the truth. She couldn't sing. Grace could barely talk.

As soon as she tried to make words, the gasping sound that came out caused her to cough. She might be sick if she couldn't stop coughing.

Charles walked away, moving out of her sight. He resumed singing, raising his voice half an octave to sing her lines.

> "Once the fun died down,
> Once you went astray,
> Once I ran to hunt things so far away.
> The stars upon the night, Disappeared from sight:
> It was true.
> It was true."

He returned, continuing to sing. Charles came to the side of the bed she was on, but she was still facing away from him. His singing stopped and he touched her bare shoulder. "Gracie, you need to turn over. I have some water for you."

Why couldn't he just untie her?

Oh yeah, he's gone freaking crazy!

He would get angry if she asked.

Grace did her best to roll over, trying not to lose the covers that hid her nudity. Not that it mattered anymore.

Charles must've cleaned her up last night.

Grace was mortified, but had to still find humor in the situation.

He had to clean up my...

She shook her head, trying to get back to the moment.

Charles had water, which she desperately needed. There was something she needed more.

His trust.

He helped her to sit up; placing the extra pillows behind her back. They were on the floor, so he must've tossed them there. Charles averted his eyes as he pulled the covers up a little higher, keeping her breasts from being exposed.

Surprise washed over her, but she took it as a good sign. He'd probably been a gentleman the night before.

"Take a sip, but go slow. We don't want a repeat of last night, do we?"

She flushed, her cheeks hot. Maybe she wasn't over the non-voluntary shower after all. Anger coursed through her veins.

Grace sipped the water, and wanted to bark, but she checked herself before she spoke, her voice still raspy. "If you'd untied me and gave me a moment to use the restroom, it wouldn't have been a problem."

Instead of being angry, like she expected, he laughed.

"There's my Grace! My little spitfire."

"I'm sorry. Please, Charles. Untie me."

He laughed again. "I can't do that."

"Why? I can't go anywhere. I'm exhausted and sore; I couldn't even walk out of here."

He sighed, set the glass of water on the nightstand and left the room.

Grace tried calling him back, but it only caused a new fit of coughs. She looked over at the glass of water longingly. Would her throat ever recover?

She closed her eyes and rested her head back on the pillows.

He was moving around in her apartment again. Was he looking for something? What? Most of the place was packed up. He was complaining to himself and it sounded like...tossing things around.

"Damn it, Grace!"

What now?

Charles was standing at the bedroom door, her cellphone in one hand, and a hammer in the other. "We need to do something about this," he said, holding them both up.

"What?" she gasped. Her heart thumped harder.

"He keeps calling, Grace. I can't have him calling my girl."

Her heart stuttered in its frantic pattering. Hope dashed her fear.

Blaze was still trying to get a hold of her.

Charles bounded to her nightstand and set the phone down. He held the hammer high.

"Charles, no! If you break my phone, he'll still call. But it'll go straight to voicemail. Don't you think he'd find another way to get a hold of me? Do you want him to come here?" Her voice cracked as she tried to get his attention.

As soon as she said it, she wished she hadn't.

That was exactly what *Grace* wanted to happen, for Blaze to come to rescue her.

"You're right," he said, and picked up the phone.

"What's your passcode?"

"Charles, please," she begged.

"What's the fucking passcode?" his voice full of venom.

"I don't have one," she whispered in defeat.

Her costar touched the screen to light it up before sticking the device right in front of her face.

The phone *clicked* as it unlocked.

Grace watched as he flipped through her phone, finding the messages icon.

Moments later he spoke slowly as he typed out the words. "Leave...me...alone...I...don't...want...you...anymore."

He set the phone on the nightstand, raised the hammer, and brought it back down with tremendous force, shattering not only the phone, but her hopes of any chance of escape.

CHAPTER 22

Blaze looked at his phone on the table in front of him and sighed. He picked it up and lit up the screen, looking for the hundredth time to see if he'd missed a call or a text. He cursed under his breath and tossed it back on the table, the sound of it reverberating through the otherwise silent room.

He'd been trying to get a hold of Grace for over three hours.

There'd been no replies from her.

He got up and paced the length of his living room, the sun setting in the huge bay windows beside him.

Blaze stopped and studied the breathtaking colors painting the sky. He couldn't enjoy the beauty, like he normally when it was on display.

Like an idiot, in front of hundreds of people on set, and possibly millions of fans watching TV and on the Internet, he'd confessed his love.

What the fuck was I thinking?

A thousand different scenarios went through his head as he waited for her to call back. Blaze reminded himself Grace had a lot to overcome with her fear of loving someone and he dropped the biggest bomb on her. *He* loved her.

I wasn't thinking. She said she wouldn't miss it for the world. I was too excited. I had to share.

He'd left multiple voice messages, and a dozen texts.

Blaze could call her again, but she might let it go to voicemail.

Again.

"Damn it! I'm a fucking bad boy, not some pansy ass bitch! I shouldn't be getting so paranoid over this!" His voice bounced off the walls in his living room, coming back at him. He took a breath and plopped down on his soft leather couch.

What did I do?

If she wouldn't answer him, maybe she'd talked to Hope? Girls always looped their best friends into what was going on in their heads. Right?

He snatched his phone up and sent a text message to Nick.

I gotta question for you, call me.

He waited twenty minutes with no reply. His buddy was usually prompt at replying. Blaze tried again.

Bro, can you ask Hope if she's heard from Grace?

After an hour he felt like it was ridiculous texting again like a worried parent again, but something didn't feel right.

I can't get a hold of her and I'm freaking out. I shouldn't have confessed on TV.

Finally, after over two hours of pacing, sitting, pacing, his phone *dinged* a reply. He almost knocked his phone to the floor in the rush to grab it off the table.

It was from Nick, not Grace.

Hope says get your panties out of a wad. Grace is probably asleep. Try again in the morning. Shutting my phone off now.

Not the answer he was seeking, but maybe they were right.

Grace was an hour ahead, and she *could* be recovering from the night they'd had before she left. She hadn't slept at all that night.

Hell, he hadn't.

Holding her in his arms after her big reveal had been an eye opener for him.

Blaze tried not to think about all the hearts he'd broken; more than he could count, because he, too, had been broken once.

Not by a lover, but by a parent who'd abandoned him at a young age. He, too, swore to never love.

Sex had been all he'd needed in his life. He'd watched some of his bandmates fall in love, get married, and have kids, convinced —at the time—that he'd never want that.

Until he met Grace.

I can see myself with her. It's more than just sex. There's a connection.

He chuckled and headed to the kitchen. "That sounds like the lyric to a song. Maybe I should write them, *and* sing them."

Blaze grabbed a beer and headed back into the living room. He ripped on the TV to scroll channels; he tried not to look at the cellphone sitting face up on the table.

He failed.

🎼

BLAZE STEPPED out of the shower and wrapped a towel around his waist. He was so glad to be back in his own home, but his place seemed...off.

He'd taken his phone to bed with him, setting it on the pillow beside him. He'd hoped Grace would send him a message, and he didn't care what time it arrived. There'd been nothing. Again.

Why isn't she answering my calls? Is she really that *afraid to love or be loved?*

He'd stopped calling. Kept texting to ask her if everything was okay.

Blaze went to the sink and wiped a hand across the mirror, exposing his reflection through the collected mist. He ran his hands over his face, feeling the beginnings of hair, as he hadn't trimmed in two days. He sighed. Needed to get moving with the morning routine.

He'd lost hope regarding hearing from Grace, so he almost dropped his coffee cup when he saw a message notification. His heart tripped and he accessed it.

He read the message twice before he sat on the edge of his bed. He stared at his phone, the text still on his screen.

Leave me alone. I don't want you anymore.

His brain—and his heart—struggled to process it. He hated confrontation, but this time he was all for it. No matter how stupid it might've been to declare his love on national TV, he wasn't about to accept her text. She'd have to reject him to his face.

Blaze dialed Grace's number again, receiving only her voice-mail. "I got your text. What the hell was that about? I get it, you're scared to love. And that's okay. You don't have to love me back if you're not ready. I'm all right with that. I'm sorry about the show, but... I couldn't hold it in. Damn it, Grace. You at least owe me an explanation! Sending a weak ass text like that is a copout, don't you think? Kinda shitty considering... Just... call me, please."

He paced the whole house as he waited for her to call. She owed him that, dammit.

After getting some things done around the house to distract himself—starting a load of laundry and putting the clean dishes away—he called Grace again.

"What the fuck... Why am I putting myself out there like this... shit..." Blaze disconnected the call, wishing he could go back and delete it.

After two hours, he couldn't take it anymore.

"Hey, Nick, I know you're about to take Hope to the airport, but I need some help." He might not share blood with Nick, but the guy was his brother, and had never let him down. He was also much better with women than Blaze.

"What's up, bro?"

"I've been patient waiting for Grace to call me back. I quit calling her but I sent her another text. I got a reply while I was in the shower. 'Leave me alone. I don't want you anymore.'"

"Seriously?"

"I don't get it, I thought she'd be happy I told everyone—the whole freaking world—I was in love with her. Don't chicks normally dig that?"

Nick laughed. "Yeah, sure, but Grace is different from anyone you've ever dated. If you're really concerned, I'll see what Hope thinks. Call you back in a few."

It seems like the longest fifteen minutes of his life. Finally, his phone rang.

He almost dropped it in his rush to answer the call.

"Hope was already boarded when you called. But I could talk to her. She said it doesn't sound like Grace. She said if Grace has a problem with you, she'd tell you to your face, or at least over the phone. Hope's certain she wouldn't send a text like that."

Blaze sighed. "Not that I'd ever call Hope a liar, but this came from Grace's number. So unless someone's there with her, she sent it." He was trying to hold back his hurt and confusion. Or was it anger?

Had she fooled him? Grace had seemed so genuine when they were together. She'd gotten under his skin almost immediately, and sex had never been so good for him. But it was more than the physical. He fucking loved her.

"Hope said she would try and call Grace. See if she can find out what's going on. She'll call me back as soon as she lands."

"I tried calling after I got the message. It went straight to voicemail. Did Hope say she had a landline?" His frustration was building but it tried to keep it from his voice.

"She didn't. But if you can't wait the three hours for her to land in Pasco, there is someone who'd know how to get a hold of her."

"Yeah, her boss. I don't know why I didn't think of him first," Blaze said.

"Good idea, but not who I was thinking." Nick's voice sounded off, like something might be wrong. Had he hesitated?

"Who?" He tried not to make it sound like a demand.

"My brother. They spent five months together. Not together-together, but you know what I mean."

Now he heard frustration. What the hell could that mean?

They both knew of Charles's devotion to Grace and Blaze didn't want to bring it up—or the odd feeling mentioning his buddy's little brother caused in his gut.

Charles wouldn't? Would he?

"I think you're right, Blaze. I'll pick you up and go to the theater with you. They can at least tell us if they've heard from her."

The smell of fresh paint assaulted Blaze when he and Nick entered the theater being renovated. Unlike the previous time they'd there, this time people met them.

He assumed they were part of the restoration crew; not a single one looked like they were in a position to give the answers they needed.

"We're here to see," Nick shot him a glance. "What's his name?"

"I think one was John or Jason. Yeah, Jason. I think the other guy was... Richard?" Blaze asked, looking at one of the crew.

"Richard's the guy that owns this place," the shortest one spoke up. "But he ain't here. Ain't nobody named Jason here, neither."

Blaze stood a little bit taller. He didn't like the way this guy was talking to them. He ignored the little man looked at the tallest guy. "Do you know when Richard will be back? Or how I can get in contact with him? It's urgent."

"He won't be back in until tomorrow. He gets here around ten, and is out before one. Check back tomorrow."

"Can't you call him, or get a number for me," Blaze asked, trying to keep his anger in check.

"Unless it's for official business, it ain't your business. And you don't look official."

His face flushed with heat, his hands tightening into fists.

"Thanks you for your help." Nick grabbed his arm and pulled him toward the door. "Come on, let's get out here. I'll call my brother in the car."

Blaze fought a weakness in his knees and tried to ignore how his gut churned.

Could something really be wrong?

Maybe Grace wasn't mad at him? Could Hope be right, and the message from her phone wasn't from *her*?

What the hell is happening?

"Dude, would you stop that?" Nick barked.

They were back in Nick's Beemer, and Blaze thrummed his fingers across his knees. "Sorry, I'm just...I dunno, nervous I guess." He couldn't voice his fear that something had happened to Grace.

"I've never seen you get so worked up over a girl."

"She's just not any girl. She's great. She's *the* girl, and I'm not gonna let her go without a fight."

Nick held up a finger up to silence him. He had his cell to his ear, but Blaze could still hear the voicemail kick in.

This is Chuck. Leave a message at the beep.

His buddy hung up and dialed again.

Three times it rang, and went to voicemail.

"Hold on, let me try someone else." Nick scrolled through his contact list

Again, Blaze was close enough to hear. Angel answered the phone after just two rings.

"Hey, sis, sorry to bug you, but I'm trying to get a hold of Charles."

"Did you try his cell?" she asked.

"Yes. No answer. That's why I'm calling you."

"Well, I don't know what to tell you, I haven't seen Charles since Tuesday night."

"Charles, what have you done?" Blaze heard his friend whisper.

CHAPTER 23

To say Grace was humiliated didn't even come close to the horrifying way she felt.

Charles had been kind enough to keep the blanket tucked up against her because he refused to untie her so she could get dressed, and *she* refused to let him dress her.

He sat on the edge of the bed facing her; spoon feeding her chicken noodle soup. He hadn't chosen it because she was feeling sick, although she was, but not the way that would require chicken noodle soup.

There was little choice of food in her kitchen. She hadn't been home in months so there was no need to have a stocked fridge and pantry. She'd had take-out since coming back.

Grace had fought him when he'd first tried to feed her, she didn't want to rely on him for anything. She only capitulated because she needed her strength if she had any hope of fighting him off if the time came.

He was being sweet, so there were remnants of her old friend. He was in control of the situation, and still kept her bound.

They weren't friends anymore.

He was...crazy.

Throughout the day she'd begged him to release her, to no avail. Most of the time he acted as if he hadn't restrained her.

Charles babbled away as if this was all a picnic, although she wasn't listening to a word.

She was obsessing on about the text he'd sent Blaze.

Grace imagined all the scenarios that result from message, of course focusing on the worst ones. She hadn't wanted a relationship before she'd met Blaze, but she had fallen in love with him.

Oh my God... I swore I wouldn't, but damn it. I can't deny it either!

Instead of being sad, it made her angry. Rage boiled her blood. She couldn't let it go. Blaze and Charles both swirled on a loop of chaos in her head. She stayed centered on the injustice of her situation.

Why didn't Blaze know something was wrong?

She was angry with him not coming for her. Rationality tried to get her to refocus on Charles's entrapment. The hours went on and she was still trapped in a place she used to consider home, Grace just felt more desperate, more hopeless.

Grace would have to save herself.

Charles scooped up another spoonful and brought it to her face, but she closed her mouth and looked away from him.

She could feel the tears of frustration burning and she didn't want him to see her cry.

"Come on, Gracie, you need another bite." He tapped the spoon against her lips.

She snapped around, spilling the soup and glaring. "What you want Charles? Why the hell are you tormenting me?" Tears spilled and she cursed. She hadn't wanted to cry in front of him.

She wanted to be strong and brave.

Sobs racked her frame, and Grace rolled away best she could, trying to bury her face into her pillow.

Charles set the bowl on the nightstand and moved toward her. He gently grabbed her shoulders and pulled her against his chest. He wrapped his arms around her.

"Get off me," she growled. "If you've ever cared about me you'd get out of here, and leave me alone."

He pulled away as if she'd slapped him, dropping her back to the pillow.

Grace kept her face averted. She couldn't look at him and the crazy sadness in his brown eyes.

Charles sighed, and cupped her cheek, tugging so she'd look at him. "That's why I'm here Gracie, because I love you. I'm here to take care of you, forever."

Grace couldn't stop crying, and *that* pissed her off.

He did not understand what love was, or what it meant to care about someone.

This was not love.

It was a weird, twisted fascination with the idea of love.

She closed her eyes and sucked in air. Tried to stop the tears, but more slid down her cheeks.

The mattress shifted. The heat of his body coming closer told Grace Charles had leaned forward.

His lips touched her cheek and a shudder snaked around her spine. The kiss had wiped the tear away.

In any other situation it would've been a sweet gesture, but he made her feel dirty.

Her body reacted before her brain did.

Grace recoiled, rearing her head back, then swung forward in full force.

Their skulls collided. Agony exploded in her forehead. She heard a crack and prayed it wasn't her.

I hope that hurt him as much as it hurt me!

Charles flew off the bed.

He had his hands over his nose and blood seeped from beneath his fingers.

She'd made a huge mistake.

"You fucking bitch! My nose was already broken!"

Grace had only a fraction of a second to brace herself.

His bloodied hand came at her face. He backhanded her, and her head flew to the left, wrenching her neck.

Pain made her eyes go white before her vision refocused, but her forehead still throbbed, too.

His words rocked her just as much. Fear spiked, and her heart took off, rebounding against her ribcage.

Charles never cussed, but the hatred he spewed sent chills down her spine.

"Stupid fucking whore! I tried to help you and you broke my fucking nose, *again*! You'll pay for this! If you can't love me like I love you, I gonna..."

He ranted in the bathroom, his words muffled by the running water from the sink.

She understood the message all the same.

Charles was about to go over the edge.

Grace took a deep breath. This was her chance.

He'd no doubt be in the bathroom for a while, so she had to move fast. She needed to talk to keep his attention while she worked on her escape. "Charles? I'm so sorry! It was an accident. I was caught off guard. I didn't mean it." She kept her voice gentle, but with enough volume to be heard over the water.

She worked to get her hands under her butt to slip her legs through. She needed to get the tape off her ankles.

Grace kept her eyes glued to the ajar bathroom door while she worked at the sticky constraints. Her skin was stuck and she lost some layers. It stung, discomfort shooting up to her knees.

She bit back whimpers; couldn't get caught. When she got it all off, the need to run made her limbs tingle.

She was still naked, but if there was a chance to get away, Grace didn't care.

She heard the water shut and leaned back against the pillows, keeping her legs close together, as if her ankles were still bound. She held her breath as she waited for him to exit the bathroom.

Her heart ticked harder, making her temples pound with every second he failed to appear.

This was the only chance she'd get. Grace threw the covers off, jumped from the bed, and ran for the front door.

THE AIR RUSHED out of her with a *whoosh*. Her back slammed to the hardwood floor near her front door. Grace hadn't heard Charles behind her

He grabbed her hair and threw her to the floor.

Charles crouched over her, straddling her abdomen, and putting all his weight on her.

She could barely breathe. Let alone move.

Grace stared into his dark brown eyes, fearful for her life.

He was insane. His eyes were wide, whites showing, his face was red, and his hair stood on end. He still had blood on his face, now brown and dry. The corners of his eyes were purple; Blaze's previous impact was green bruising.

The intensity in his gaze sent terror all over her body. Tremors chased each other down her spine, spreading to her limbs until she shook all over, even her teeth chattered.

She tried not to show it.

Her bound hands were bent at the elbow and resting across her chest, hiding her nudity. She was grateful she'd managed to avoid them being trapped beneath Charles.

He roared with the first punch, and every one after, screaming how hurt he was that she tried to run from him when he loved her so.

Grace tried to block the blows with her hands, despite them being bound, but it didn't lessen the pummeling.

He gave her no quarter as he hit her, rocking her body as he kept her trapped under him.

The pain was excruciating and she could no longer see as he punched her face again.

He was going to kill her.

Part of Grace wished for that, warring with her survival instincts.

She just wanted it all to stop.

Her unfocused vision went black, and blessed darkness welcomed her.

NICK SLID onto the brown leather sofa while Blaze paced his living room. Their open beers sat untouched on the coffee table.

"You can't get a hold of your brother. I can't get ahold of Grace. Hope says something isn't right. Are you fucking kidding me?" He stopped his jerky movements long enough to pick up his drink. He brought it to his lips but never took a sip. "He's obsessed with her. Remember our fight?" Blaze raged, setting the warming bottle back down, falling back into pacing.

"I know..." His friend frowned, and he could feel his frustration.

"I have to do something."

"We have obligations," Nick reminded him. "You can't miss the Jimmy Kimmel taping. Besides, you don't know something's really wrong."

"Fuck that, man. This is Grace. Answer me honestly. Would he hurt her?"

His longtime friend looked torn, as if he didn't know. Or didn't want to tell Blaze what he really thought. Nick cursed. "I don't know..." he whispered.

He cursed, too. "Look, I know he's your brother, but she's my..." *the love of my life* was about to come out of his mouth, but he didn't want to say it.

Hopelessness washed over him, and when they made eye contact, it was in Nick's expression, too.

"I don't know what he's capable of, but I know he thinks he actually loves her," his friend confessed.

"One thing I learned from Grace, everyone sees love a little different. The difference is, how to show it."

Nick's cell rang. "Shit, it's Angel."

Blaze stilled when his friend put the phone on speaker.

"Hey, sis."

"Nicky? Did you ever get a hold of Charles? I'm getting worried."

Nick snapped his head up, looking Blaze in the eyes as he spoke.

"No."

"Oh. Well, damn."

"Angel. What's up…" he prompted.

"He was acting all funny. I don't know, like he was high or something. He wasn't. I can always tell when he's fallen off the wagon and this isn't it. He just kept walking around the house, in a constant circle, mumbling something about roses."

Blaze shook his head. What the hell could that mean? It couldn't be good.

"Did he say anything else, before he left?" Nick pushed.

"I didn't even know he'd left! When I went to bed, he was still leaving tracks in the kitchen. I woke up about nine a.m. and he was gone. No note, no goodbye. Nothing. Nicky, I'm worried. You don't think he's relapsing, do you?"

His buddy sighed. "I don't think this is drugs. But keep trying to get a hold of him. And let me know if you do." He set his phone down on the couch beside him after disconnecting the call.

"That's it. I have to get to her. I need to get to Denver."

Nick stepped right up to Blaze, his hands on his shoulders, grounding him. "Try and get some sleep. There's nothing you can do tonight. Tomorrow we can reach out to Richard, or Jason and see what they know. If it comes down to it, we can fly out tomorrow night, together. Just slow down, dude." He grabbed his cell and headed for the front door. "I'll call you in the morning."

He shut the door behind his friend, securing the lock. He pulled his shoulders back and said the words he'd wanted to say to his friend, but didn't. "Give my regards to Jimmy. I'm heading to Denver."

BLAZE PULLED his lucky green canvas bag from the closet and stuffed it full of clothes, not paying attention to what he grabbed. He jumped on his laptop and looked for flights.

He wasn't having much luck finding one that would get him there fast enough. They all left too late in the afternoon. His best bet would be going directly to the airline counter.

In his rush to get to Grace, he let one small fact slip his mind.

Shit! I still have no idea where I'm going!

He stared at his laptop a moment, unsure what to do.

I'm a fucking idiot. Google that bitch...

Blaze opened a search engine on the phone and looked up 'Majestic Theater, Los Angeles'. He didn't expect that to work, but sure enough, there was a website for the theater.

He scrolled through the black and white images of the old theater, only skimming over the information about the remodel.

At the bottom was a link for *Contact Us*. He could taste the hope in the back of his throat as he touched it. Another page popped up with the address, email and...

Thank God! A phone number.

Blaze pressed his finger more aggressively than needed to initiate the call. He held his breath as it rang once, twice, a third time, before going to voicemail. Fear road him as he left a message. "Good evening. I'm sure you won't get this until morning but I'm looking for Richard. Or Jason. I'm sorry I don't know last names. This is Blaze, I'm Grace's..." *boyfriend, lover, what the fuck am I?* "Friend. I'm afraid something might've happened to her. Can you please call me back, or call her, or something. I just need to make sure she's okay. I'm flying to Denver in the morning, if you can send me her address, I'd appreciate it." He left his cell number and hung up.

Damnit. I sound like I'm the fucking stalker... you don't know me but can you tell me where she lives? Fuck!

CHAPTER 24

HER WHOLE BODY WAS MADE OF AGONY. SHE COULDN'T OPEN HER eyes, and when she tried, white-hot daggers shot into her head. They were swollen shut. Her cheekbones hurt, and her temples pulsed.

Grace wished unconsciousness would claim her again.

She wanted to cry, but didn't think she could. Her left wrist was also offering pain. Was it broken?

She swallowed, and it also answered with discomfort. So dry. Like a desert.

Her hands were still taped together, so she couldn't inspect it to see what was wrong.

Grace didn't want to think about where she was or what was happening, but Charles was all around her, assaulting every sense but sight.

They were still sitting on the hardwood, and her head rested on his shoulder. The heat of his arms was around her, and something wet dripped onto her naked shoulder.

Was that a tear? His or mine?

He stroked her hair and crooned in her ear, his voice no

longer sounding like the maniac he'd been moments before. He was soft and gentle.

What a contradiction.

"I'm so sorry, Grace. Why did you make me do this? I love you. Why can't you love me back?"

It took her a moment before she could find her voice. She cleared her throat to try again, and pain bit back; made her wince. "Charles, this isn't love." Her throat was more than raw, and her voice was barely a whisper; but he'd heard her.

He went quiet and stilled; halting his rocking as if he needed to do so to hear better.

"You don't beat people you love." Grace didn't care if she made him angry anymore. He'd already damaged her, if he was going to kill her; nothing she said would change that. Rage boiled her blood and wiped the caution from her words. "What's wrong with you? There's a special place in hell for people like you!"

She still didn't attempt to open her eyes. She didn't need to see.

Charles' whole body tensed before shoving her from his arms.

Grace couldn't stop her momentum. Her head slammed the floor. More agony exploded behind her swollen eyes. She curled into the fetal position. Since her eyes were close, her other senses seemed heightened.

He must've scrambled to his feet, because he paced beside her; his feet angry clomps on the floor of her apartment. "All I wanted to do was love you. Why is it so hard for you to do that? Why can't you just love me? I just want to be loved!"

GRACE HAD LAIN in a ball on the cold hardwood floor listening to Charles pace for what seemed like hours.

At some point, she heard him slumped to the floor—she assumed leaning on the front door. It sounded like he had his head between his knees as he sobbed, because his cries went in and out, sometimes muffled.

That made regret settle over her. Was her old friend in there somewhere?

No.

Not after what he did to me.

She needed a distraction, so she tried to concentrate on things that made her happy like the sounds of thundering applause from an audience.

She could only hear *him*.

Grace tried remember the warmth of the stage lights caressing her skin.

She was cold.

It wasn't just her body that was broken and bleeding.

It was her heart; her soul.

Grace focused on the sound in the room. Something changed.

Charles's crying had subsided and now it sounded like he was asleep. Deep even breathing greeted her ears.

She tried to open her swollen crusted eyes.

Her vision went in and out as she tried to blink to clear it, but it hurt too badly. She swallowed a gasp, because she didn't want to wake him.

She could see, but not very well.

The little light in the room came from the lamp on the coffee table, next to her couch. It was night, but she had no clue what time.

Grace lifted her head to confirm Charles was indeed asleep.

He was blocking her only way out.

Charles had destroyed her cellphone, leaving her with no way to communicate outside of the apartment. His phone was always in his back pocket.

She had no chance of getting it. Even if she did, was it as easy to open as hers? Or would she need a code?

No. His phone's not even an option.

Banging on the walls wouldn't gain attention; and would likely wake him.

Grace only had one chance to turn the tables.

I can get up, take a shower, get dressed, and try to act like it's any other day.

Charles was fragile. She could manipulate him into thinking he was still in control. It was dangerous, but it might be the only way she'd survive this.

Grace's hands were still bound and already on the floor. She pushed down, trying to ease into a position. White-hot daggers snaked up her left wrist. It had to be broken. Through her limited vision, she could see the swelling.

I can't let it stop me from what needed to be done.

It took her a few minutes—and a few tries—to stand. She had to use furniture and the wall to get her to the bathroom.

Grace shut the bathroom door silently, and sat on the edge of the tub. She was almost afraid to start the water; she didn't want him to wake up.

Warm water cascading over her sore body would help a lot. The idea made the decision for her, and she reached for the faucet.

She held her breath, waiting for him to come storming into the bathroom, but as the hot water rushed out, and the door did not open, she let her shoulders loosen.

Grace used her teeth to bite the packing tape off her wrists. It took what seemed like a thousand years, but she was finally free. The skin was red and raw, but she was glad to move her hands. She could finally evaluate her wrist.

It was swollen and black and blue around the joint. A test movement resulted in pain. Grace hissed and cradled the wrist against her body, but her time was limited.

With her good hand, she switched the water flow to the shower-head and climbed into the tub. When she tried to stand, her hips and legs protested, so she slid down into the tub and pulled her knees to her chest. Everything hurt.

She let the hot water heat her to her core before she attempted to wash her hair with her right hand. The smell of her shampoo and body wash was oddly comforting. It reminded her of Blaze.

Blaze.

Would she ever see him again?

With her forehead resting on her knees, Grace let it all out. She cried until there was nothing left. Exhaustion took over and she dozed off.

FREEZING WATER BROUGHT GRACE AWAKE.

She'd fallen asleep in the bathtub before, but this was different.

With no neighbors on her floor, the hot water lasted so much longer than the normal twenty minutes. She looked down at her pruned fingers. How long *had* she been in there?

Despite the cold, she had to step out of her little piece of sanctuary in this new world of madness. Just like washing her hair, she learned it was a little difficult to dry off with a broken wrist.

She was grateful she hadn't had a chance to completely pack up the bathroom before Charles had showed up. She opened the medicine cabinets and found an ace bandage. She wrapped her broken wrist the best she could, hoping it would relieve some pain.

Grace wiped at the steam on the mirror, finally getting a chance to see her face.

Is that really me?

She gingerly touched the goose egg on the side of her head where the remote had left its mark. There was a gash running right through the center. The shower had cleaned the remaining dried blood away.

The deep, dark coloring of the bruises covering most of her face had her stomach ready to turn on its end.

She had to break away before the sight got the best of her.

Grace steeled herself, then opened the bathroom door, expecting to see Charles up and moving.

He was still passed out up against the front door.

She stood there a moment taking in the sight of him; the morning light shining down on him from the space where the red curtains were parted.

The neck and front center of his gray T-shirt was covered in blood, most of it from his nose.

Was any of it was hers?

His head was slumped to the side, his blond hair looking dirty and unkempt. One clump tried to cover his eyes but the deep purple stained the green remnants from the previous break. Bloodied knuckles rested against the floor.

She released a quiet sigh before turning her back and heading to her bedroom, into her closet for some clothes. She'd never been so relieved to have a pair of jeans on than she was at that moment.

Her stomach grumbled and she crossed her hands over her abdomen to block out the sound. She's hardly consumed anything last two days. She tiptoed to the kitchen and tried to find something to eat. There wasn't much in her cupboards or fridge, and she didn't want any more chicken soup. She grabbed a box she'd neglected to pack, and smiled.

This'll work.

There was also coffee.

That would definitely wake Charles, but she'd have to face him eventually. Maybe he'd think she'd done the food for him.

Grace got a pot brewing and started the pancakes. She didn't have bacon or eggs to go with them, but that was okay. Pancakes were a comfort food, and she could use all the comfort she could get, even if it was a simple meal.

It was difficult working with one hand, so she had to use her left elbow to get it done.

Of course, the smell of coffee and food woke Charles. She could hear him moving about, followed by a loud yawn.

She glanced at the clock on the microwave. It was already after nine am. She'd already survived over forty hours with him; she could make it a few more to turn the tables. She smiled as he stepped into her tiny kitchen. "I hope you're hungry. I think I made too much." She was proud of herself; she'd hid her fear pretty well.

Grace had to gain control, even if he thought he still had it.

His expression was relaxed as he moved closer.

Her first small victory.

Charles gently ran his knuckle over her blackened cheek. He said nothing, but leaned in and brushed his lips over her bruises.

Grace held back a cringe—from physical discomfort as well as not wanting to give herself away, and she managed a weak smile for him.

She opened the cupboard above her head and grabbed a mug, handing it to him.

He poured himself some coffee and moved to the table. Still didn't speak, but that was okay with her.

She brought him a plate and joined him. She kept herself busy with eating so she didn't have to comment, either.

I will get away from him, one way or another.

CHAPTER 25

BLAZE GLANCED AT THE CLOCK; IT WAS 4:23 A.M. HE'D TRIED TO sleep, drifting off a handful of times in the few hours he'd been in bed. His eyes always bolted back open. His stomach wrenched, so that didn't help matters.

What has she done to me?

He understood where Grace was coming from, never wanting to love or be loved. There was too much pain involved. So how did he, a confirmed heartbreaker, end up the one with a broken heart?

Blaze dozed off again, but it didn't last long.

She never left his mind.

He obsessed over the last time they'd made love—every touch, every kiss, every movement, and every drop of sweat. It was real, as if stamped on behinds eyes. It brought him comfort.

There was no way Grace wouldn't want him in her life.

It didn't matter if his love-confession had been public.

She hadn't sent that message.

Something had happened.

Something bad.

Something that had something to do with Charles.

That rat bastard.

Blaze crawled out of bed to get a drink, but found himself pacing again.

He'd known Charles for more than half his life, and had seen him on tons of roller coasters.

The guy had a crazy streak.

He'd stood by the family through three bouts of drug rehab; but never once had he shown signs of violent tendencies.

That doesn't mean they are not there.

He might not have seen Charles around Grace for any length of time, but what he'd seen was…concerning.

After all, the idiot had attacked *him*, fought with him, and shouted that "she's mine" crap. Then, the kid had only seen a very small amount of PDA.

I wonder what he'd done if he knew I'd been between Grace's…

Blaze shook his head, clearing the crude thought away. He had more respect for Grace than that. Charles just pissed him off. He *believed* Grace didn't feel that way about Nick's younger brother.

Had her rejection shot him over the edge?

Would Charles hurt her?

The more he thought about Charles, the more worried he got.

I've got to do something…

Soon enough, Blaze was leaving his bedroom, the green canvas bag slung over his shoulder. He snatched his keys on the coffee table next to the couch. He hurried to his car, stowed his bag and pulled out of the driveway.

Guilt stirred in his gut.

Nick would be by his side for this, but their manager would want him dead for not showing up for the Jimmy Kimmel show.

I can't get Nick busted as well. I'll deal with the consequences, later.

Getting to Grace was more important, no matter what.

He stared at the clock on the dashboard while he sped down the highway. He hoping the ticket counter would be open.

It was already 6:30 a.m..

Is Grace still sleeping? Or is she getting up now and make herself some breakfast?

He imagined her in a tiny little kitchen, barefoot, music playing in the background, as she danced around the room collecting the ingredients she'd need to make herself something to eat.

Blaze smiled.

Until he thought about the truth, or what could be the truth. Grace was most likely not alone. She wouldn't be singing to herself, songs of love and happiness.

She could be hurting… she could be…

No! Can't think like that!

He turned on the radio, trying to drown his morbid thoughts.

Blaze found himself singing along. The song was from the '80s. It made him think of Grace.

Journey's, *Faithfully.*

The lyrics hit a little too close to home. They got stuck in his throat, and he choked back tears.

How had this woman gotten so deep under his skin in such a short amount of time?

He hadn't been looking for love, hell, he wasn't even convinced he believed in it.

Until he'd met Grace.

Blaze pulled into the airport and parked in the closest stall. He didn't care if it was in the fifty dollar a day lot.

He needed to get inside and on a flight, fast.

The band had access to a charter plane when they were out together, but he'd never tried to get it just for himself. Besides, if he tried, he'd have to go through management and they'd find out he was skipping town, *and* the Jimmy Kimmel Show.

He stepped up the first airline counter he saw, Delta.

"Good Morning," the overly cheerful redheaded agent greeted. "How may I help you?"

"I need to get to Denver, immediately. What do you have?"

"Yes, sir. Are you looking to fly today, then?"

"Isn't that what I said?" He took a deep breath. He didn't need to be an asshole to this poor girl. "I'm sorry. I'm just in a hurry. Family emergency. I really need to get to Denver on your first flight."

She asked for his ID and after looking it over, popped her head up and stared, as if she was seeing him for the first time. "Oh! You're from..." she stuttered.

"*Razor's Edge*, yes. Can you get me on a flight?" He tried not to get irritated with her again, but damn. Now was not the time to have a fangirl moment.

He watched her cheeks flush red, matching her hair, as she ticked away quickly on her keyboard. Before he'd met Grace, this would've been one moment he used his fame. He could have flirted with this woman so intensely, he'd not only walk away with what he needed, but her panties in his hands as well.

You're not that man anymore....

"I'm sorry, but I have nothing that would get you there today. But I can see that American Airlines has a few standby seats available for the ten-forty-five. I can't book it for you, but I'll call down to Stacey and let her know you're on your way. Head down that way," she pointed to his left. "It's about fifteen ticket counters down."

"Thank you," he said, ripping his ID from her hand as he bolted away.

Blaze tapped his foot in irritation as he waited to get through security. Even with TSA Pre-Check, the line was ridiculously long. He tossed his canvas bag on the X-ray conveyor belt and stepped up to the body scanner, waiting to be called through.

He continued forward, through the archway; the alarm buzzed and he was sent back.

Damn! Stupid belt buckle!

His gem incrusted skull buckle he always wore was quickly removed and tossed on the conveyor. He stepped through again.

Buzz.

Once again he was returned to the other side.

"Sir? Did you remove your cellphone, keys, watch?" The agent drilled him.

"Yes, yes." Blaze tried to hold his building anger in check.

"It maybe your boots. Are they steel toed?"

He cursed at himself. Why hadn't *he* thought of that?

He rushed to untie them, getting the long laces knotted up. Blaze wrenched at his foot, trying to yank the boot off, without finishing loosening them.

He almost fell over.

Blaze made it through without another irritating buzz. He collected his things, found a bench to sit on, and began the painstaking task of detangling the mess he had made.

Finally he sat at his gate, keeping his head low, waiting for them to start boarding.

He almost jumped out of his skin when his phone blared. He struggled to get it out of his back pocket, almost missing a call from Nick.

"What the hell, dude? You leave in the middle of the night and don't tell anyone? Did nothing I say last night sink in?"

He tried to interrupt, but it was best to let Nick get the yelling out of the way. "I'm sorry. I couldn't sleep. I had to do something."

"And you couldn't wait until after the goddamn taping to get a flight out? You left me to explain to not only management, but our brothers, why you didn't bother to show up! Not fucking cool! Scott is freaking out; you know how he is, big brother and all. And what about Hope?"

He opened his mouth to defend himself, but Nick didn't pause.

"Attention guests in the terminal, we will begin..."

"Bro, I can't hear you. I'll call when I land." Blaze didn't let his friend get another word in.

He sat in the back of the plane, and Blaze kept turning his phone on and off in irritation.

They'd been sitting on the tarmac for over an hour. The stifling heat in the cabin was getting to be too much.

His head was hurting, tears pricking his eyes. He rubbed at his temples, trying to ease the discomfort.

"Ladies and Gentlemen, our sincerest apologies on this delay. We are having a minor mechanic malfunction, but a crew is on their way to assess. At this time we're unable to have the cool air on, so we will be coming through the cabin with water for you. Thank you for understanding."

Blaze gritted his teeth.

There was nothing he could do, but sit there and wait. He turned his phone back on and sent his best friend a text.

Bro, stuck on the tarmac. Are you done taping yet?

They'd likely rehearse from ten until noon, break for an hour, then film from one to three.

He'd be in Denver by that time.

Hopefully.

"Ladies and Gentlemen, it appears we are unable to pressurize the cabin. We will be returning to the gate and relocating you to another aircraft."

Well, shit.

CHAPTER 26

CHARLES WOKE TO THE SCENT OF FRESH BREWED COFFEE. HE rolled his shoulders forward, stretching his sore back before he attempted to stand.

It took him a moment, sleeping on the floor upright had left his legs numb. The tingling sensation of blood running through them gave him a moment of pause.

When he could finally stand, he went straight to the kitchen, yawning as he went. His heart soared to see her flitting about, his love making breakfast.

The smile she gave him warmed his heart

He couldn't help but touch the beautiful creature that belonged to him, and *only* him.

Charles caressed her cheek; gave a soft kiss to say good morning. He wanted to kiss more of her but the rumbling of his stomach reminded him he needed food.

And coffee.

After filling the cup she gifted him, he made his way to the table to wait for her to serve him. The pancakes smelled delicious and his mouth salivated at the thought of consuming them.

He'd just put his third pancake on the plate when there was a hard knock at the door. He glared at Grace, telling her to stay silent.

He rose from the table, grabbed a knife from the block on the counter, and headed to the door. He left the chain in place, so it only opened about two inches. He glanced back at Grace one more time, tilting the knife back and forth.

Her leery expression told him she'd gotten the message; *don't even think about it.*

"Can I help you?" He took on a character that moment, sounding like any sane man would.

"I'm looking for Ms. Harrison," an older gentleman replied.

"She's indisposed. May I help you?"

"I'm Mark, a friend of Jason Pope. He asked me to check in on Ms. Harrison. Make sure she made it home safe. Sounds like she's got a busy week, with packing and all. Thought I'd offer my help."

Charles smiled, giving him the full range of his acting abilities, despite the churning in his stomach. "I appreciate you stopping by and I'll make sure to thank Jason. But Gracie has me, and we're just fine."

"Please tell her I'm here. I'd love to meet her. Jason has spoke of her often and I'd like to match a face to the name. Speaking of which; you are…?"

He glared at the intruder.

This is Jason's friend? Not likely...

The portly man was at least ten years Jason's senior. His bland brown hair was seriously receding, his belly said he liked beer over water, and he'd look as likely to step into a theater as a moose.

However, he had to finish the charade, make the man go away.

"I'm her husband. She's in the shower; it's been a long trip home. I appreciate your dropping by, but as you can see, all is well."

The moment Charles began talking, he heard Grace get up and start moving closer to the door.

She was so close.

Too close.

He had to get this man to leave.

Immediately.

When he tried to close the door, the man stuck his foot in, preventing Charles from ending their conversation.

"Mr. Harrison. It doesn't appear as all is well. What happened to your face?"

He chuckled and touched his broken nose. "I fell down the stairs trying to carry all our luggage up here last night. I'm sure you noticed the broken elevator."

The older man gave a polite smile, finally believing the lies. "Indeed I did. Quite a hike for this old man. Well, get that looked at. I'm sure it hurts."

Grace didn't get any farther.

Charles grabbed her wrist, the broken one, before she could get on the other side of the door.

"Thank you." He shut the door and locked it. He turned on her with anger fueling him. "What the hell do you think you are doing?"

Grace touched his cheek, like she used to when he was upset about something. It just infuriated him more.

Instead of putting his hand over hers, he dropped the knife onto the small entry rug, grabbed her other wrist and pulled her hand down. He held both her wrists together.

"I was just wondering who stopped by. I never get visitors," she stammered.

"You wanted him to see you!" His vision flashed red. He fought the desire to strangle her for lying.

"No! That's why I stayed behind you, so he couldn't see me. Promise!"

He gripped her tighter, trying to control on his anger.

"I swear, Charles, I was just curious."

"Why would he come here? Who was he?"

She lowered her voice to just above a whisper. "I don't know who he was, Charles. That's why I was coming to look. No one would check on me. I only have you. You're the only one who cares about me."

Her voice carried her sincerity.

"Can we please finish our breakfast? The pancakes are getting cold."

He still held her wrists tight in his hands, and had control over them. Charles pulled her closer, so when their bodies met their hands were trapped between them.

In the space of a breath, he leaned forward and stole her lips.

His kiss started out soft, but didn't stay that way. He let go of her broken wrist, to run his fingers up her lush body, skimming across her full breasts, up her throat, to rest at the nape of her neck. Then he buried his grip in her hair.

His cock hardened when his mouth demanded more, trying to coax her lips apart to deepen the kiss.

She opened her mouth and gave him the access he so richly desired.

Charles took her acceptance, the kissing became more aggressive, more severe.

He needed her.

His body was calling to hers, and damn did it hurt.

Charles took his hands out of her hair and stepped back, desire fueling his next steps. He whirled toward her bedroom, pulling her along. His jeans were becoming far too tight. He had to get them off, and get Grace naked, too.

"Charles," she whispered, pulling him to a stop.

"It's okay, Grace. I won't hurt you."

"Charles," she said again. "I need to finish breakfast."

He brought her hand to his lips and tried to kiss her knuckles as he maintained his grip on her. "I'll be all the breakfast you need." He waggled his eyebrows suggestively.

"I'm sure you could be, on any other day." She reached to touch his cheek again.

His hand went over hers.

"But I've hardly had any food the past few days, and I just don't have anything in me. Please, let's finish eating. We have all day to play."

Charles let out a sigh.

She's right. Later... when I am more awake. So I can thoroughly enjoy torturing her body. And making her scream.

He smiled and they returned to the table.

GRACE QUIETLY WORKED in the kitchen, taking all the time she could cleaning up from breakfast. Working with a broken wrist was to an advantage, despite the pain. She couldn't have moved faster if she'd wanted to.

Charles had offered to help, since she was doing it one-handed, but she refused, stating it was women's work and he should make himself comfortable in the living room.

He'd turned on the TV, complaining about not being able to find something to watch as he scrolled. She murmured something appropriate and was relieved he didn't come back to the kitchen.

She reconsidered how she could get away.

Charles had been her dearest friend, and just about every-thing that came to mind made her cringe. Even if he'd hurt her already. She didn't want to hurt him.

It just wasn't in her to cause another pain. She had to come up with something else.

Grace wanted to listen to music while she cleaned up, if

nothing else to distract her from the pain, but Charles had broken her phone, so she had to go without.

She tried to think of something to sing quietly, something to help her stay calm, but nothing came to her. She didn't want to sing anything from *The Splendids*; that would get Charles' attention immediately.

That damned play!

If Maddie and Louis had been any other roles, would Charles still have fallen?

What he was feeling wasn't love, but the residual effects of their characters and *their* passion.

I never meant to hurt Charles, and if I could do things again, I'd be more cautious with how I treated him.

She had told him from day one there could be nothing more than friendship. She'd never meant to lead him on. There was no going back. Just forward.

Which brought her back to the present.

Who was the man who'd been at the door?

She had no one to come check on her. Maybe Hope? Could the older man be an old family friend? That didn't seem right. All of Hope's family lived closer to the West coast.

What about Blaze...

Did he believe the text? Did he give up on me? No! He said he loved me, even after I told him my past...

She could kick herself for not telling him her address, but she hadn't thought there'd been a need.

He'll try and find me, right?

Using her shoulder, Grace wiped at an escaped tear. She went back to her dishes, trying to force Blaze from her mind.

> "Let me mend your broken heart, let me wipe your
> tears,
> My life is tied to yours; we've waited all these years.

Let me mend your broken heart; let me wipe your
tears.
My life is tied to yours; we've waited all these
years."

The words filled her mind as she put the dishes away. They
were lyrics from the only *Razor's Edge* song she could remember.
She found herself humming the melody.

The more she tried to push Blaze from her mind, the harder
the memories came back.

Grace saw his chocolate eyes when she closed hers, felt his
warm kisses on her neck. She inhaled, trying to steady herself.

It wasn't the heady scent of Blaze that filled her senses, but
the musk-filled cologne of Charles.

He came up behind her, sliding his hands around her waist to
rest on her belly. He leaned in, leaving little kisses on her
shoulder and neck. "What were you humming, my love?" Charles
asked into her ear.

Ice shot down her spine, and Grace froze. She was once again
in a rough position.

She'd been thinking about Blaze and her body was alive, but
went cold when Charles spoke.

She kept putting the silverware away as he held on to her.
"Just something I heard on the radio once. I only could remember
part, but it's stuck in my head."

He kissed her shoulder again. "Hum some of it for me, maybe
I know it."

Grace's heart raced. She drew a blank on any modern-day
song she could replace it with.

She could only hear Blaze.

"It's all right, it doesn't matter," she tried.

"Please, Gracie. I wanna know what filled your mind so
intensely you didn't hear me call to you from the other room,"
Charles said.

Her stomach lurched, bile filling her throat. She had to swallow deep to keep it from rising.

He was jealous of not only his brother, but Blaze. Saying her lover's name would send him into a rage that would only result in more fists in her face, if not another broken bone.

She had to get things back in her favor.

Grace girded her loins and turned in his arms, slipping her own around his neck. Ignoring her heaving stomach, she pasted on a smile. "Really, it doesn't matter, I can't even remember anymore. Now that you're here." She forced her voice to be sweet, borderline seductive. This was just another role to play.

Charles wanted this so badly, he couldn't see it was just a rouse.

Grace prayed, anyway.

He kissed her once, then twice, keeping them soft. He smiled and pulled back ever so slightly. "I'm sorry I hurt you, Gracie. I never meant to hurt you." He sounded sad as he released her.

Her hands slipped down from his neck and he reached to touch her swollen eye.

"Does it hurt?"

She tried not to scoff. Her swollen eyes were the least of her worries. The broken wrist was more of a priority. All she could do was a nod.

"Do you have anything, like Aspirin, you can take?"

"I think I have some aspirin in the bathroom." In a cabinet in the bathroom, where she had her bandages, there was medication.

Not only Aspirin, but Hydrocodone. She'd gotten it when she'd torn three ligaments in her foot and ankle. She hadn't taken many of them so the bottle had more than enough.

If she could get her hands on them, maybe Grace could find a way to drug Charles.

They always made her sleepy, so hopefully, they would do the same to him. If she did a double or triple dose, it would have to work, and not kill him. Three pills wouldn't be an overdose, right?

"Thanks for the idea. I'll get them," she said and headed that way, moving before he could stop her.

Charles was right on her heels. He caught her hand right before her fingers closed around it. "Let me help you," he said in a sweet tone that made her want to cringe.

Grace heard the underlying tone in his voice.

"We don't want you to do anything to hurt yourself further, do we?" He smiled, and she wanted to narrow her eyes, but didn't.

Don't make him angry. Maintain control, she chanted to herself.

He opened the bottle, taking one precious pill out. "Open up," he said, offering her the pill.

"Charles, I can't swallow pills without something to drink. Can you go to the kitchen and grab me a glass of water?"

He wasn't as stupid as she'd hoped.

There was a small glass for rinsing her mouth right next to the sink.

He stepped over to fill it, turning his back to her for a brief moment. He'd taken the bottle with him.

Dammit!

Grace glanced in the cabinet and with a swift hand, grabbed the purse-sized bottle of extended-release Tylenol PM he'd overlooked.

Maybe it would be better than Hydrocodone. It was for sleeping, after all.

She shoved it in her front pocket right in time for Charles to present her with the water.

He offered her the pill again, but she shook her head.

She hurt, a lot. Under normal circumstances she'd take the whole thing. They made her sleepy, and *that* would be worse than the pain she felt.

"Just half, please. Can you break it?"

He did so without argument, placing the other half back in the bottle. Charles didn't return the bottle to the cabinet, and ushered them out of the bathroom.

She cursed him silently, but was relieved to have a contingency. Grace headed back to the kitchen, still a few more dishes to put away.

Charles pulled her to a stop, bringing her in close again. "Where did we leave off?" He leaned in to kiss her again.

Nerves flittered in her stomach. She needed to get away from him. "We left off with me putting dishes away," she teased, praying it sounded convincing.

"Dishes can wait; I can't." His voice was husky and full of desire.

She swallowed, fighting the urge to wretch. "Charles... Um, not to be insensitive but..."

She needed more time.

Grace had a plan, but it was too soon. So she'd need to make time. "It's been a while since you, ah, showered."

His cheeks flushed pink.

Thank God he realized she was right.

He didn't answer, but started back toward the bathroom, taking her with him. He still clutched her good hand.

She'd been foolish to consider he'd leave her alone to take a shower.

Dammit.

Still holding on to her, Charles leaned into the bath and started the water. He stuck his hand in, testing the temperature. When he looked back at her, he was smiling.

It made her sick.

"Are you gonna join me?" He sounded sincere, and she fought not to show the way he made her feel.

"Oh, I wish I could but..." Grace held up her bandaged wrist. "I just don't think it's a good idea to get this wet. But I can go get started on some lunch. I know it's early, but I'm hungry, again."

So was Charles, but not for food. He let go of her wrist and reached for the hem of her shirt. "It'll dry. Come, join me."

Her heart shot into overdrive. He had to buy what she was selling. She pulled on her acting skills and prayed. Grace playfully tapped his hand away and giggled a sound so fake in her own ears. "I already had a bath this morning. I don't want my skin to dry out. But the water is hot; you should get in before it runs cold."

He touched her cheek before walking around her to go into the living room.

Grace followed hesitatingly.

Charles stopped at the coffee table beside her couch and picked up the roll of packing tape and the scissors. He waved the tape at her. "Well, if you won't join me, you'll have to just get comfy sitting on the toilet."

Grace bit back a gasp.

Is he serious?

She looked into his dark brown eyes. "Charles, you don't have to do this." Her protest died as he plopped her down on the toilet lid.

"Yes, Gracie. I do. You'll understand soon, I know you will. Now put your hand up here." He indicated the towel rack hanging on the wall above the toilet.

"Charles, please," she tried.

He grabbed her right hand, the good one, and pulled it up towards the rack. "Do it, Grace! Grab it!"

She didn't want to, didn't want to give him control again, but she had to stay focused.

Grace had to keep what little trust she'd earned, if her plan was to work. She blew out a breath and grabbed the towel rack.

CHAPTER 27

GRACE TRIED TO MOVE HER FINGERS AS THE BLOOD RUSHED OUT OF them and they were numbing.

Charles had taped both her hands to the towel rack and the broken wrist was screaming.

This was the only time she wished she had a cheap towel rack.

Once, she'd slipped while getting out of the shower, and had grabbed the rack. It'd pulled it right out of the wall.

When she'd replaced it, she used industrial drywall screws with steel anchors and rustic looking pipes. *Nothing* would pull this out of the wall.

She sighed, wishing Charles would hurry.

Wait. Never mind.

Grace would have to connive another way to stave him off. His lustful looks as he'd gotten undressed really threatened her gag reflex.

There was a reason half the cast had wanted to bed Charles. Aside from his charismatic personality, he had a body to die for. He had a few tattoos hidden when on stage. They usually kept him in long sleeve shirts to keep those large ones from sight.

His pecs and abs would tempt most women, and he had broad shoulders and a slim waist.

He's an example of looks being deceiving for sure.

He'd undressed with no hint of shyness, displaying his features, including a happy trail.

Of course, she could appreciate a man with an appealing form, but not Charles.

Not after what he'd done to her.

She hadn't averted her gaze; she'd looked at him with what she'd hoped he'd seen as challenge, but with her luck, he probably thought she wanted him.

Never.

Charles moaned in pleasure under the hot water. A moment later he stuck his head out from behind the shower curtain, and their eyes met. "You sure you don't want to join me? I hear this shower has a two occupancy minimum."

Grace's heart slammed into her throat. Hadn't she and Blaze had a similar conversation just days before?

"Actually, sweetie. My meds are kicking in, and I'm having a hard time staying awake."

"Then you should get in here. The hot water will help."

He was being persistent, but she wasn't about to give in.

"I appreciate that, but it'd just make me even sleepier. I probably should go lay down for a while." She had a game plan, the perfect idea to get out of the apartment and away from Charles without hurting him, but it had to be a little later in the day.

Grace had to come up with something to fill the time she needed; other than what *Charles* had in mind.

That would never happen.

She played over and over in her head what she'd do, and he began singing show tunes.

"Sing with me, Gracie, I love the sound of our voices entwined."

Her throat was still shot from everything she'd been through;

she worried it would never heal, so singing was out of the question. She didn't want to make him angry, so she hung her head like she'd fallen asleep. Grace heard him move the curtain.

"Oh, my sweet Grace," Charles whispered.

She stayed as still as she could when the water shut off. She was exhausted and could easily sleep for real, not because of the medication, but the sheer fatigue from the past two days coming down on her.

"Gracie, love." He worked the tape off her hands. "Baby, wake up. Let's get you to bed."

Grace batted her eyes a few times, as if to remove the sleep.

Charles only had a pink towel slung low on his waist. Rivulets dotted his tawny chest. His chest was just a breath away from her face, as he continued to remove the massive amounts of tape he had used to keep her in place. He smelled like her body wash; a scent that'd comforted her earlier. Right now, it turned her stomach.

She looked up at him, trying to keep the sleepy hazy appearance in her eyes.

He must've seen something else; because he leaned down for a kiss.

Grace faked a yawn, causing him to pull back. She didn't want to face him again, so she hung her head in exhaustion, only to get an unfortunate glimpse of Charles below the waist.

The towel sat low, revealing the curve of his hip bones and more. He was getting an erection.

She closed her eyes again. She had to get out this situation.

Charles removed the tape and was rubbing her right hand, soothing the irritated skin.

When he reached for the left one, the broken one, she snatched it away.

"Please don't touch it, Charles; it really hurts. The meds are kicking in and I need to lie down."

He stepped back and helped her stand, but he didn't relinquish her arm. Instead, he walked her walk to her bedroom, Grace leaning against him for fake support.

Charles let her go and she climbed onto the bed.

She curled up on her right side, her face away from the door. Grace was afraid she'd would fall asleep if she wasn't careful. She wanted to sleep, but she couldn't afford it.

"I'll be right back, love. I just need to go start my laundry." He leaned over and kissed her cheek.

She stared at the wall. What time was it? Her clock was missing.

Grace had been making breakfast just after 9 am. So between their unexpected visitor, doing the dishes, and Charles' shower, it had to be sometime around eleven.

If she could just stay in the bed for an hour or two, it would be lunchtime, and she could implement her plan.

She went over things again, trying to stay awake, but sheer exhaustion won out.

HIS HANDS WERE warm and tender and he gently kneaded her swollen breasts, taking a moment to tempt her nipples to hard pink tips.

Oh, how they had ached for his touch.

She could feel the heat pool in her lower regions. She could feel the heat of his body pressed against her back, his swollen arousal making its presence known.

Her body came to life as his magic hands caressed every part of her he could reach, running a tip of a finger on the underside of one breast, then the other, before moving to tease her stomach.

It seemed like forever since he'd touched her that way.

His hands continued to move even lower, reaching the most sensitive part of her, bringing her body to a point of no return.

The pressure was building within before the explosion. She wanted to see his face as he took her to the edge.

She faced him, her eyes still closed in pleasure.

As she slowly opened them...

GRACE GASPED. She jarred awake from her dream of Blaze, only to find Charles in the bed with her.

He was naked.

The erection she'd felt in her dream had been *his*.

Her shirt and bra were pushed up, exposing her breasts. Her cheeks flush hot. Not with arousal.

With rage.

Had her dream been Charles taking advantage of her unconsciousness?

Was he the one to bring my body to life?

She shuddered.

No.

She didn't want his touch; she never had. But the thought of such without her consent had her in knots.

Her guts churned, like they had earlier. She was going to vomit.

In one swift movement, she pushed him away, jumped off the bed and ran to the bathroom.

Grace just made it to the toilet in time to lose everything her stomach had held, which wasn't much.

She was still heaving when Charles came up behind her and put his hand on her back, rubbing small circles around, trying to comfort her.

Tears streamed down her face.

How could he do that to me?

She kept trying to tell herself he hadn't really touched her, she'd been dreaming after all, but her shirt was out of place. She hadn't fixed it, but now, in between heaves, righted herself.

Grace began crying then.

The sobs racked her body as she grabbed the edges of the

toilet bowl, trying to push the feelings of his hands on her, far from her mind.

Charles moved to the sink to get a wet washcloth wet.

She flushed and tried to stand up, but lost her balance and fell on her backside.

Instead of helping her up, he laughed. "That's my Gracie!"

She narrowed her eyes and shot daggers at him, but he didn't see it.

He offered her a hand.

Grace reached for it; she couldn't get up on her own.

Charles pulled her upright, but the movement was too fast and she got dizzy, seeing stars, and she almost fell into his arms.

"I've got you." His voice was sweet, and he kissed the top of her head. "Do you wanna go back to bed?"

"*No!*" She didn't mean to scream it, but *bed* was the last place she wanted to be with *him*.

He studied her face, and his eyes glinted with a hardness she hadn't seen since she'd turned the tables.

Grace's heart skipped and she swallowed. Tried to smile. "I think I need to eat something. Taking medication on an empty stomach did me in." She slipped from his embrace and left the bathroom.

It was now or never. Time to try and get free.

Please, let this work.

BLAZE WAS aghast at his shitty luck. It'd taken nearly an hour to get the plane back to the gate and unloaded. Being in the back of an overheated cabin had almost done him in. He was ready to hop in his car and drive there.

I'd get there faster at this rate.

The airline rerouted everyone to another gate, but the new plane wouldn't be taking off until 3:30pm.

The crowd erupted into argumentative voices, many sharing their deep concerns over missed connections and displacements.

He was among them, but there was nothing he could do. Blaze had to wait, like everyone else, to get on the new flight.

He walked to the new gate, an unpleasant sensation engulfing his stomach. He put a hand over his abdomen. Maybe he just needed to eat something. He hadn't had food in almost twenty-four hours.

Blaze picked the first restaurant closest to his new gate, wavering on whether or not he should have a beer, but discarded the idea. He was hungry but found himself picking at the burger, more than eating it.

Can three-thirty just get here already?

He paid his check and joined the other disgruntled passengers.

The two hour flight felt like a lifetime.

Would it be easier if she doesn't want me? Or finding her with Charles? He wouldn't hurt Grace... would he?

Blaze pulled his phone out of his back pocket, eager to turn it back on the moment the plane's wheels had hit the ground. It powered up and pinged with alerts. There were numerous texts from management, which he ignored, and a few voicemails, one was from Nick.

"You're probably in the air but I wanted to let you know, soon as we finish on Jimmy I'm heading to the airport. Already have a car lined up. I just need you to text me the address. Bro, it's not for you. I mean, it is. But I promised Hope I'd do everything I could."

Good thing. I will *kill Charles if he has hurt her. In* any *way.*

The next voicemail made his stomach clench tight. It was Richard.

"Thank you for your call. I'm glad our Grace has such good friends. I've tried to reach out to her, to no avail. It went to her voicemail. Jason said he's got a golfing buddy that lives out that way. Woke him up, but he said he'd be glad to check on her. In the meantime, let me get you her address."

He's worried too.

Blaze could hear it in his voice.

There was also another voicemail from Richard.

"All right, Mark stopped and said everything's okay. But I'm hesitant to think so. I left a message with Jason to call me back. His buddy said Grace's husband answered the door and said all's good. I was under the impression she wasn't married. I'm very glad you're headed that way. I'm becoming worried. Please, let me know when you arrive."

Charles!

Blaze pushed his way off the plane, not waiting for the people in the rows in front of him to exit, nor did her care if people thought he was rude. He practically ran though the terminal, cursing that the damn train was taking too long. It was the only way to get from the terminal to the main building.

The bile rose in his throat as he waited to get a taxi. Blaze wanted to bowl over everyone and jump in the first one that drove up, but there was a security office helping direct travelers.

Finally in the back of an old smelling yellow cab, he barked the address to the driver. "Hurry!"

It was almost six p.m. and he was worried about what he was about to walk into.

Worried?

No.

He was *scared.*

Charles had never physically hurt a girlfriend before. So...he wouldn't hurt Grace, would he?

His phone rang and he looked down to see Nick's number. "I've landed, obviously, and I'm waiting for my rental. What's your ETA and where am I going?"

"I'm in a cab; we just left the airport. Damn, I wish I'd known when you were landing. We should get there about the same time, if you can drive faster than this dipshit is. Thank God. I need you there, because I don't know what I'll do to Charles if he's hurt her."

"I know, I'm right there with you. I don't know what'll happen next. But I'm sure Grace is okay. She seems like a strong woman. But Charles. He's been acting weird, the lashing out; I hope he hasn't started using again. My brother's been clean for almost a year now. Drugs make people unstable and known to do things they otherwise wouldn't." Nick was scared, too. His voice wavered.

No doubt it was for his brother, as well as Grace. Hell, he was probably scared for him, too.

"I gotta let you go; I need to set up my GPS. I'll see you there."

"Thanks, Nick."

"Dude, don't go in without me. *Promise*."

It wouldn't end well if Blaze went in alone.

"Then you better fly like the wind."

CHAPTER 28

GRACE PULLED THE LEFTOVER CHINESE FOOD OUT OF THE FRIDGE, along with the bottle of wine.

It broke her heart that this special bottle of wine she'd held on to for so long, saved for that special occasion, was now being served to her captor; just after he'd had assaulted her in her sleep.

However, it also would be what saved her.

He sat on the couch, scrolling through the guide, trying to find a movie.

She'd convinced him that after being ill from the medication she'd taken, that nothing sounded better than some food, wine, and curling up on the couch with him and a good flick.

Charles wasn't having any luck finding something he liked, and was getting agitated.

She suggested he look through the box of movies she'd recently packed up, right beside the entertainment center and not sealed yet.

He looked through the box, making more noise than a kid with wooden blocks

Grace had dished out one plate of food and placed it in the microwave. As it rotated, she poured two glasses of wine. She listened carefully to make sure he was still rummaging the movies.

She pulled the small bottle from her pocket and took four pills out. She planned to crush them and put them in his food and wine.

Her first idea was put it all in the wine but if he tasted the slight bitterness of the Tylenol PM in the wine, he might set it down and not drink it.

If she put it in the food too, he was more likely to consume all four. She needed him to take that.

Crushing them would make noise she didn't want Charles to hear, so she watched the time count down on the microwave.

She got a spoon ready. The moment the timer *binged*, she crushed the pills. Then swept it all up into her hands, dropping some into the glass of wine, and putting the rest into the Sesame Chicken and rice, stirring it all in.

Grace swished the wine around, watching the crushed pills dissipate within the liquid. She finished preparing her own plate before taking Charles his.

"Pick one of these." He gestured to three DVDs, as she handed him his plate.

"Oh, I don't care, I love all my movies. You can pick." She went back to the kitchen to grab his wine.

Damn, only having one working hand sucked. It took her three trips to bring everything out.

She sat on the far left side of the couch and Charles loaded the movie of his choice. She ate her food very slowly, using her upset stomach as an excuse.

Normally Tylenol PM took about 45 minutes to work, but she prayed it kicked in faster; the bottle stated not to chew or crush it.

She wasn't expecting the movie he'd chosen and it caught her off guard.

Win a Date with Tad Hamilton.

Could he have picked a more obvious title? It was about a small town girl who won a date with a handsome Hollywood star. Her best friend, who happened to be the boy next door, was hopelessly and secretly in love with her.

She'd always loved the movie, but at that moment, it brought her so much anguish. Grace kept glancing at Charles, trying to see if he'd eaten his food, but he was too wrapped up in the movie. She picked up her glass of wine and touched his leg to get his attention. "Charles, sweetie, this is a very special glass of wine."

He looked at her suspiciously.

She caught the look and ignored it. "I bought this bottle at a little vineyard in Walla Walla, Washington, and I've been holding on to it for a while now, saving it for a special occasion."

He smiled, turned to the coffee table, and picked up his glass.

"When I bought it, I didn't know what that would be. At first, I almost opened it when I got the part of Maddie. But it didn't seem right. Then, when I got home the other day and found your roses, I knew the time was right to open this bottle." She tilted her glass toward him.

"Here is to us, and to many more scenes together." He brought his glass to hers and they clinked them together. Before she took a sip, Charles leaned forward, clearly wanting their lips to meet, as well.

She gathered her courage and followed suit, letting their mouths brush before pulling back. Grace upended the glass, drinking it all in one gulp.

Luckily, he did the same. "Maybe we should do a little rehearsing," he teased. "I think our stage kiss could use some work. I do believe you once told me I wasn't kissing you right." He leaned over and slipped his hands into her hair, gripping her head so he'd have better control. He brought them together, tempting her mouth to open so their tongues could dance.

Grace was grateful her stomach grumbled right at that moment.

They broke apart laughing.

"All right, I'll let you finish eating lunch, but..." Charles waggled his finger in front of her face. "I'm taking care of dessert."

She fought a cringe. If things worked out, he'd be passed out before the movie was halfway over.

"Would you like another glass of wine," she asked about twenty minutes later.

They'd finished their food but Charles was showing no signs of drowsiness.

Grace tried to ignore encroaching panic. Maybe the Tylenol PM wasn't as effective because he still had some drugs in his system. She had no clue what he'd taken the first night he'd come but it was something bad, like heroin or meth.

She just didn't know enough about drug abuse to have any real idea. So she figured one more Tylenol PM shouldn't hurt him.

She stood up, grabbed her glass then reached for his.

"I normally don't drink much," he said. "But since we're celebrating, I guess one more wouldn't hurt."

She smiled, her first real smile in days. Grace returned to the kitchen and poured more wine. She was just about to pull the small bottle from her pocket when he joined her in the kitchen.

"So what're we drinki..." Charles wobbled and grabbed for the wall for balance. "Gracie... I don't feel so good. Grace...what... did... you... do?" His words slurred.

"Nothing, sweetie. I'm just getting us more wine. Come on, back to the couch. We have a movie to watch." She didn't bother adding more medication. She walked around him, setting his wine on the table before coming back for her own.

He stood in the same spot, still gripping the wall for support.

"It's my turn. Let me help you." She stepped next to him and Charles put an arm around her shoulders.

It took all her strength to get him to the couch.

He fell with a great harrumph.

Grace helped get him settled on the couch in the correct position. She wanted to run but he was still conscious enough to stop her.

She needed to wait until he was fully passed out.

Just a few more minutes!

She could play along just a little longer, then she'd be free.

Grace sat beside him and he slipped his left hand onto her thigh, gripping tight, as if to hold her in place. She put her hand over his, so she would feel him relax, and it'd give her a better idea of when to bolt.

She waited until the movie was over.

His grip hadn't lightened. His head was against the couch like he was sleeping.

She started to get up, and his fingers dug into her thigh. She couldn't stop a cry from shock and pain.

His head snapped up. "Whatcha doing, Gracie?" Charles was no longer slurring, but still sounded out of it.

"The movie ended, I was just going to put in another one. Any suggestions?" Grace did her best to hold back tears. She'd been so sure this would work, so sure she'd be running down the stairs of her apartment by now.

He finally let go of her thigh and sighed. "I picked out three I liked, so put one of those in."

She got up and looked over at the pile. The films were all rom-coms like the last one.

Charles was clearly trying to say something with his choice of movies.

Grace reached to the pile, not bothering to look at what movie. It didn't matter. As she got it into the DVD player and closed it, she glanced back over at Charles.

His head was leaning back against the couch again.

She held her breath and started toward the front door.

Charles hadn't moved yet, his breathing was shallow, so she kept on her path.

She'd just lifted the chain on the door when the opening credits started, blaring the theme music of the studio house.

His head shot up.

With a few curses, Grace dashed to the couch, curling up next to him as if she'd never left. She put her left hand on his chest as if nothing was amiss, ignoring the pain in her wrist. "I love this movie, I am so glad you picked it," she said.

"What movie?" Sleep coated his voice, making it thicker.

She hadn't bothered to look. Luck was on her side, and as the movie began the lead actor's name came on-screen. Patrick Dempsey. *Made of Honor.*

"Oh." Charles' eyes slid closed again.

Grace trailed her fingers up and down his chest and stomach, hoping it would lull him to sleep.

Instead of helping him sleep, it was helping him in other ways.

She snatched her hand back, praying the erection would go away.

"Don't stop Gracie; that feels really good."

Will he ever fall asleep? Jesus!

Grace didn't want to encourage him, so she waited a few moments to see if he'd fall asleep on his own.

Charles tried reaching for her, still not opening his eyes.

She gave up and put her hand back on his chest. Every time she stopped, he'd call her back to him.

Not quite halfway through the movie, she couldn't take it anymore.

Grace eased off the couch and he reached for her.

She was expecting it and moved before he could get a grip on any part of her. "Go back to sleep, sweetie, I'm just going to the bathroom," she said in a sing-song voice.

He put his hand back down and she slowly slid to the front door, which was nowhere near the direction of the bathroom.

Grace had her hand on the lock when she heard his voice.

It wasn't from the couch.

Charles was right behind her.

"Where do you think you're going?"

CHAPTER 29

GRACE'S HEART STUTTERED AND TRIPPED. SHE COULD TASTE THE fear in her throat. She had to come up with something in a hurry.

She faced him, her hand still on the doorknob. "Sweetie, I was just going to get the mail. The office manager will start to worry if I don't come down. We don't want Jeanette getting into our business, do we?"

Apparently, Charles didn't agree with her 'perfect' excuse.

"Quit ...calling... me... sweetie," he screamed. "If she saw your face she'd be all up in our business in two seconds!"

She played stupid. "What's wrong with my face? I mean, I didn't put on any makeup today. Heck, I haven't even looked in a mirror in a few days."

Charles touched her cheek ever so gently and sighed. "I hurt you, Gracie. I didn't mean to, but you made me do it. You made me hurt the one thing I love most in this world." He slipped his hand further back so he could delve his fingers into her hair. He stepped closer so he could take control of her mouth.

Grace kissed him back but focused on her right hand, which was still on the doorknob, her fingers curled around it tightly.

She brought her left hand up, cringing at the pain in her wrist as she slid her fingers over his abs, continuing until it came to rest close to his heart.

Charles pulled her in tighter, wrapping his left arm around her waist, pressing their bodies together.

She shivered as his erection pressed against his jeans to torment her thigh.

What she had to do next would hurt, bad.

Grace pressed on his chest, partially to get his attention, but also because her wrist hurt. "Charles," She tried to get him to take a step back away from her.

He pressed his forehead to hers but didn't let her go.

"Charles," she said again.

There must've been something in her voice, because he finally stepped back enough to look at her.

His hand left her hair, trailed down her cheek again. His thumb caressed her bottom lip before he looked into her eyes.

"I'm really sorry," Grace said before doing the one thing he'd never imagine. She brought her knee up hard and swift, connecting with his fully aroused groin.

Charles hit the ground with a thud, and a slew of cuss words.

She tried her hardest to get the door open.

Then threw it wide with gusto and ran for the stairs.

He grabbed her ankle and yanked back, and she fell forward.

Grace screamed as her broken wrist took the brunt of the fall; her physical agony was outweighed by her pure anguish of his grip on her, her loss of freedom before it could really be.

She rolled over, using her elbows to hold her up.

Charles began dragging her back into the apartment.

She screamed, tearing her vocal cords, but this might be her only chance for someone to hear her.

The sound was barely above a whisper.

It did no good.

Grace tried to kick at him with her free foot but he just grabbed it too, and continued to pull her in.

All the while, he was still on the floor, whatever pain she'd inflicted clearly not holding him back.

As she got to the door, she grabbed onto the frame with all her might. Her left wrist hollered, but she held on.

Her broken bone be damned.

If he got the door closed with her inside; that was the end for her.

The rage in his dark eyes promised death.

Charles had her by the waist now and wouldn't let go.

She was mostly inside now, her hands on the doorframe were all that was left. Grace glanced around, trying to see if there was anything she could hit him with, like a lamp, or even a pair of her high heel shoes.

Charles was on his knees, looking as if he was having a hard time moving. He was still a thousand times stronger than her.

She pulled as hard as she could, trying to get just a little bit more of her body through the door. Grace let go of the frame with only her left hand, reaching over to the small colorful rug next to the door where she put her shoes when she came home.

The knife Charles dropped.

She wrapped her fingers around the handle, and swung the knife towards Charles.

It sank deep into the muscle on his upper thigh.

He screamed and her let go.

She had the length of a breath to scoot out of the room, trying to pull herself up with the doorframe. She didn't stay to see if he pulled the blade from his leg.

Grace ran as fast as she could for the stairs, taking them two at a time.

"Grace!" Charles screamed her name over and over. "Grace! Come back!"

. . .

SHE KEPT RUNNING DOWN, but tripped as she turned the corner of the stairwell, wrenching her left ankle as she went down.

Grace slipped at least three steps before she could right herself. Sharp edges scraped down her lower back as she met with the concrete steps.

She tried to stand, but agony shot through her ankle, into her calf, sending tears streaming down her face.

"Grace!"

His voice was too close.

How was he moving that fast with a knife wound?

She tried to hurry; still had three more flights to go.

He was in the stairwell above. His voice sounded like he was right behind her.

"Gracie! I know you didn't mean to hurt me. Come back, I need your help." He cajoled now; his words were sweet, like her friend seemed a hundred years ago.

Charles, her friend was no more.

All that remained was the monster that'd always hidden inside him.

Grace needed to keep going; she hobbled down, holding on to the railing on the right side, only able to take one stair at a time.

When she got to the corner, there was no railing, so she hopped, trying not to use her left side.

She'd just gotten down a few more stairs when her heart stalled.

"I found you."

It hadn't been just the stairwell projecting his voice.

Charles was standing there, at the top stair after the corner, blood running down his leg, soaking his jeans and dripping on the concrete floor.

Bloody footprints were on the stairs behind him.

"Where do you think you're going?"

Grace couldn't reply, fear caught in her throat.

She needed to keep going.

She gritted her teeth and ran, both feet hitting the concrete.

Grace screamed out her physical pain, her emotional anguish, running faster than she thought she could, pushing past the broken bones in her body.

Down she went, around another corner, down more stairs, then a third corner.

She couldn't stop, even if she wanted to.

Momentum and sheer adrenalin pushed her forward.

She would survive.

"Gracie!" His voice lingered behind her. "Grace!"

Grace reached the bottom of the stairwell, slamming into the hard metal door that separated the stairwell from the lobby.

She had nothing to stop her forward motion. She hit it so hard with her right shoulder; it dropped her to the ground.

Grace lay there in a broken puddle, crying from the distress of it all. She closed her eyes tight and sobbed.

"Grace?"

There was a bare whisper behind the door.

A trick of her mind.

"Grace, baby?"

Blaze can't be here. I'm hearing things.

"Baby? I need you to get up, please."

There was a knock against the metal.

"Grace! Wait for me. I need you! Grace," Charles called.

He was so close.

She needed to move.

She couldn't move.

"Grace, baby," the voice said from the other side. "The door's locked. We can't get to you unless you move. Please, baby, get up. I need you to... Oh God! Grace!!"

She opened her eyes as Charles came around the corner, standing at the top of the last steps.

His skin was ashen, blood covering his leg, hands, and even on his face. He took the steps one at a time, slowly, reaching out for her with a bloodied hand.

"Why would you do this, Maddie? Why would you hurt me like this? I love you, Maddie. You know I love you." Why was he calling her Maddie?

He's finally lost it. Does he think he's Louis?

"Baby! I need you to move!"

The door shook, but didn't open.

Grace couldn't take her eyes off Charles as he came closer.

"Maddie, I need you. I need your help," he said, his voice weak.

Her heart hammered in her ears. She wanted to move but was frozen.

𝄞♫

A RED HONDA pulled up beside the cab as Blaze was paying the driver.

Nick jumped out, and the vehicle jerked forward, like he'd barely put it in park.

Thank God.

Without saying a word, they dashed into the building.

The entryway looked like any other old apartment complex. To the right was a door that said "Private: Office", and to the left was a wall of mail boxes. There was an elevator next to them, with a large "Out Of Service" sign hanging fro the door.

Nick pointed to a steel metal door just down the hallway.

Blaze pushed at the door with no avail.

It was locked.

Knock, Knock. Blaze waited for someone to answer at the office door.

An attractive older gal opened it and before she said hello, racked him over from top to bottom, making him thoroughly uncomfortable.

"What can I do for you?" she crooned.

"I'm here to see *my girlfriend*, Ms. Harrison, but the stairway door seems to be locked." He emphasized his relationship with Grace.

"Oh, yeah. I had to lock it. For security. Just buzz Grace on the keypad there and she can let you in."

Before Blaze even made it over to the intercom a cold chill ran down his spine. He heard the screams of a woman.

His woman.

His gut told him it was Grace.

He ran for the stairwell door. Panic snaked around his spine and he fought it so he could move.

He needed to get to her.

Through the small rectangular window, Grace was visible. She ran down the stairs and slammed into the door, then slid to the floor.

Blaze called her name, but she didn't answer.

"Where's the fucking key?" He yelled over his shoulder as he continued to slam his shoulder on the door, fear about to bring his lunch up.

"Damn it, shove the door open!" Nick demanded.

"I don't want to hurt her!" Helplessness—and more fear— washed over Blaze.

His heart slipped to his gut, or maybe his toes—when a bloody Charles had come into view.

Calling out to Grace didn't seem to help.

He needed to get that door open.

"Here. Move," the woman said and pushed Blaze out of the way.

"I'm sorry, baby." Blaze put his full weight against the door and shoved the moment the locked clicked back. He rushed round to her side and Nick sped past him.

His friend ran straight for his brother, catching Charles as he slid to the ground.

Blaze dropped next to Grace, pulling her into his arms, tears streaming down his face. "I'll never let you go," he whispered into her hair. "I'll never let you go."

CHAPTER 30

BLAZE PACED THE LENGTH OF THE HOSPITAL ROOM, CONSTANTLY looking over at Grace to make sure she was really there.

He'd stayed by her side as the ambulance had taken her to Denver General, never releasing her right hand.

His face had been white when they'd told him in the ED he had to wait in another room as they examined her, took X-rays, and other 'things' he couldn't be a part of.

The moment they'd allowed him to join her, he'd refused to leave her again. They now were waiting for someone to come to update them on the results of her X-rays.

"Ms. Harrison," an older gentleman said as he came into the room. "I'm Doctor White. How're we feeling?"

Blaze tensed, waiting for her answer. He had asked this many times and she kept blowing him off. She wouldn't lie to the doctor, would she?

"I'm doing much better, now. Thank you. How's Charles?"

The doctor looked at Blaze, then back to Grace, clearly confused.

"Believe it or not, they were once good friends, and my Grace can't seem to stop caring about him. Even after all he did to her."

The doctor stepped took her hand in his. His gray-blue eyes catching hers. "It's very kind that you're worried about him, but let's focus on you first."

Grace shook her head. "Not until you tell me, how is he?"

He looked back at Blaze, who just nodded.

"Well, according to HIPPA I shouldn't be sharing any information with you."

Grace scoffed.

"Let's say hypothetically, a certain person lost a lot of blood, but the knife wound to his right thigh luckily only nicked the lateral circumflex artery. We found heroin in his system, which didn't help any with his blood loss. He's had surgery but we'll be watching for any possible hematoma. There were substantial muscle and tissue damage, so he'll need physical therapy. We also set his nose. He's got a bit of recovering to do. But you, my dear, have even more."

He moved to the computer on a rolling table, just to the side of her bed. The doctor grabbed the mouse before turning the screen so they both could see.

Blaze stood on the other side of her bed so he could hold her hand again, while the doctor explained all her injuries.

"Let's start at the top and work our way down, shall we. There's a large goose egg on your left temple, multiple lacerations and bruising to your face, and busted blood vessels in your eye. Your vocal cords are severely damaged. But with rest and a little help, you'll recover."

"Will I ever sing again?" Grace was almost afraid to ask.

"Yes, with time. But don't push it; you'll do more damage. There's abrasions to the skin of both wrists, the left wrist suffered a distal radial fracture. Extensive bruising on torso, minor skin abrasions on your back, and your ankle has a third-degree sprain or lateral ligament tear. Six weeks in a boot, then months of physical therapy."

Blaze let out a groan. Charles had done damage, he hadn't realized the extent.

"You're dehydrated as well, so let's keep with the IV until discharge. Now we need to talk about the worst damage of it all. The one you need to focus the most on for healing."

Blaze looked to Grace. What could he possibly be talking about?

He'd already listed to worst of it.

The doctor must've seen confused look on their faces and reached over to pat Grace's shoulder. "Your mental health. Too often it gets overlooked. Your physical health will suffer if your mental health isn't taken care of. You just went through something traumatic. It looks like you have some support."

He glanced at Blaze.

Together they turned to Grace.

"But you'll need professional help to heal, just like your bones do. Have you ever heard of Post-Traumatic Stress Disorder? It's something that will become a part of who you are. It's all right to say, I have PTSD. I've got a great doctor I'm gonna have visit with you. She'll go over some things with you and get you on the right path to healing. All right? I'll be back to check on you before I leave."

Blaze leaned down and kissed her tenderly.

He didn't take offense when she pulled back slightly.

It would take time, she had so much healing to do.

He would wipe away any trace Charles left behind.

Time... I just have her give it time.

They planned to keep Grace in the hospital for three days, mostly to keep an eye on her mental health. She kept trying to tell them she was fine, but until she was ready to accept it was okay to not be fine, they wanted to keep her.

Blaze stayed by her side, only leaving for brief periods to help finish getting her stuff ready for the move. He got movers to finish packing her things, transferred to the truck, including her furniture.

He'd insisted she let him get her stuff to California.

She was in no shape, physically or mentally to be taking on that responsibility.

Blaze had just returned from finalizing everything at her apartment and tried to hide his excitement in his smile as he walked in. His hands were behind his back, holding on to something. He stepped closer revealing it was a large gift bag. "I have something for you," he said in a sing-song voice.

She tried to sit up a little more. "Clearly," she teased back.

"I was helping with stuff in your apartment, and I found him on the floor, cowering under the bed."

He watched her face light up in pure joy as he pulled a white, pink, and orange stuffed tiger out of the gift bag.

"Frisco!" She started crying.

"I think he was hiding under the bed, waiting for you."

She snuggled the tiger close to her chest.

"Thank you," she managed between sobs.

&♪♩

ON THE SECOND day of her confinement, as Grace was calling it; Nick came to visit.

She cringed when he first walked into the room. She'd forgotten how much they looked alike, Nick and Charles.

Except their eyes; they were so very different. Not just the color, but the depths of them.

He proceeded to the side of her bed with caution. He looked to Blaze for approval before stepping closer.

She reached for him with her right hand.

"I am so sorry," he began.

"You have nothing to be sorry for," she whispered.

"But I do. If only I'd been a better brother, if only I hadn't antagonized him. I should've known from the first night I met you at the ball; he was obsessed with you. We could have prevented all this." A single tear slid down his cheek. His eyes were rimmed in red.

She gave him a gentle squeeze. "Nick, we both know this would've happened, no matter what. None of us did anything wrong. Charles needed help. He hid that, from all of us. There was no way of knowing it would come to this. But trust me, I played the 'what if game', for three days. It always came back to the same thing. Only Charles is to blame here. I hope this gets him the help he so desperately needs."

He nodded and flashed a wobbly smile. "Oh, I have something for you."

Grace cocked her head to the side.

Nick put his index finger up, then left the room.

She threw Blaze a glance to see if he had any idea what was going on.

He shrugged.

Nick held a huge bouquet of daisies. It was so big it blocked all view of him.

She tried not to laugh at the absurd amount of flowers when someone stepped around Nick.

"Hi, Elvis." Hope wiped at the tears pouring down her cheeks.

"Hope! You know, I really hate that nickname!" Grace wanted to jump from the hospital bed and run to hug her friend. That wasn't going to happen.

Her bestie rushed to her side and threw her arms around her.

Her ribs were about to break from the sheer force of their hug, neither one wanting to let go.

Hope released her and took a tentative step backward. "I'm so..."

"Do *not* say sorry! I can't hear another person say sorry!"

Her friend's mouth dropped open. She was taken aback by Grace's harshness.

"It's just... it's no one's fault. Don't be sorry. I'm just glad you're here."

"I wish I could've gotten here sooner." She sounded so sad.

"You're here now, that's all that matters."

Nick stepped up behind Hope and wrapped his arms around her protectively.

It filled Grace with happiness, to see her friends find love. She rested her head back and closed her eyes, taking in everything that'd happened.

In less than two weeks, her world had changed forever.

🎼♪♩

TWO WEEKS LATER, Grace walked into the renovated theater with a rhythmic *click, thump, click, thump*. With one high-heeled black patent leather shoe, and a walking cast, she was quite the site to see.

Jason and Richard had been kind and understanding, offering to do anything she needed to get her on the way to healing.

Her voice was slowly coming back, and she needed to get out of her new apartment.

Blaze had stayed with her every night since their arrival. He'd slept on the couch in the beginning, because Grace had a panic attack when she'd felt him lying next to her.

Every time she woke screaming, he ran to her side and held her until she fell back asleep.

Slowly, they'd worked to get her comfortable with him simply lying beside her.

She was finally realizing the extent of the damage Charles had done.

Grace still couldn't even kiss Blaze with her eyes closed.

It would take time.

He never once showed any sign of upset.

There were nights she'd laid awake, listen to his breathing, wondering when he would give up on her and leave.

Grace stepped into the auditorium and breathed it all in.

The smell of fresh paint was fading, the plastic sheets were gone, and the tools all put away.

She both feared and craved the day she'd be back on a stage, playing someone else's life.

Richard came up behind her, making a loud cough to let her know he was there.

She faced the older man, and smiled.

"Welcome back, Grace. Are you ready to start your new life?"

THE END

AFTERWORD

Were you curious what was in the drinks, 'Nick at Nite' and 'BJ in the Morning'?

Here are the drink recipes for your enjoyment… if you are of the appropriate age.

Don't be Grace, please drink responsibly.

Nick at Nite
  1.5 oz. Cuervo Gold Tequila
  1.5 oz Peach Schnapps
  4 oz Sweet and Sour Mix
  2 oz Cranberry Juice

Shake ingredients in a cocktail shaker with ice. Strain into glass

BJ in the Morning
  1 oz Malibu Rum
  1 oz Creme de Banana

1 oz Blue Curacao

1 oz Orange Juice

1 oz Pineapple Juice

Shake ingredients in a cocktail shaker with ice. Strain into glass

ALSO BY ANDREA HURTT

Undone - A Prequel Novella to Masquerade

Incomplete

SNEAK PEEK

Read on for an excerpt from
Andrea Hurtt's new novella

UNDONE

Now available from Piece of Pie Publishing

ORDER IT NOW

OR

GET IT FREE

Sign up for Andrea Hurtt's Newsletter
and get the ebook at no cost!

https://dl.bookfunnel.com/n9we1apx9k

UNDONE

CHAPTER ONE

"Breathe. Just breathe." Grace took a deep breath as she entered the community hall's recreational room. This was where she was her life-changing event?.

The lights were bright, harsh old fluorescent tube bulbs. The room smelled like a locker room.

She took in the less-than-impressive view.

The bleachers were closed and pushed up against the walls, giving the room a large cavernous feel. If anyone yelled, it would echo off the walls.

It made Grace smile.

That slice of joy only lasted a moment.

Her new costar, was about ten feet away, bouncing a red dodge ball like it was a basketball.

She cringed inside.

Those balls were made of nightmares!

"Gracie! You're here! It's about damn time! We can't get started without you. Hey! Catch!" The good looking, well-built twenty-one-year-old man threw the ball at her.

She stepped out of the way before it could collide with her. The flying red rubber hit the wall behind her only to roll back her way. Grace continued to ignore it, walking closer to not only him but the others in the room.

"Seriously, Grace. Would it really hurt that much if it hit you?" Charles crossed his bare muscled arms over his chest, looking at her with mock disapproval.

If you only knew.

She forced a smile and stood by the other actors. Grace, for all her name implied, had always been clumsy.

In middle school, they'd given her the nickname, Graceless. One time in gym class, she tried to dodge one of those red balls. She'd slipped and broke her left arm when she'd hit the wooden floor.

She'd screamed like the world had ended, and everyone had laughed. The horrible teasing was born. That was the day she lost her voice, not just physically, but emotionally. She'd become an introvert, caving in on herself.

If Grace talked with no one, no one could hurt her.

Years later, theater had helped change all that. Taking on characters, *becoming* someone else, her whole body changed.

She had poise and grace she'd never had before.

Her new addiction.

She always needed more.

"Everyone please take your seats, I don't care where. Just sit and I'll pass out the scripts," Jason, the man in charge said. He was an amazing man with a vision. At six foot, five inches, his height alone made her uncomfortable. His sun-bleached hair and copper tone shouted he spent more time outside than in a dark theater. When he smiled, and those pearly white teeth shone, it set her at ease.

Jason had been on a massive search throughout the theater communities everywhere, for actors looking to spread their wings. He needed people that could act, sing, and dance and weren't afraid to leave their homes for an extended period.

That was what'd caught her eye, and motivated her to drive the long distance to audition.

Grace took a seat next to her new costar, as she tried to push back memories she didn't need at the moment. She *had* to focus.

The script in her hand took on a permanent curved because she kept rolling it and squeezing, then unrolling and smoothing it out.

Her nerves were getting the best of her.

I still can't believe I am here. This is really happening. Mom, I'm doing it. I'm doing this for you.

The younger man bumped her shoulder, bringing her back to the moment. "Are you ready for your life to change?" he whispered in her ear, his breath warm from his earlier exertion with the damned red ball.

♪♫

ABOUT THE AUTHOR

Andrea Hurtt is an emerging author of various romance categories. She enjoys writing a little bit of everything.

She's still deciding what she wants to be when she grows up. Andrea has been a dental assistant, a stay at home mom, owned her own clothing store, was a clothing designer with a vintage inspired clothing line, Amaryllis Designs, even won Omaha Fashion Week for Top Designer in her category, and Top Boutique for Cancer Survivor Night.

Andrea currently spends her days either writing books or making #EmotionalSupportPillows and traveling around the USA and parts of Canada with the cast and fans of the CW TV show Supernatural.

She is the mother or two children, two cats, two dogs, and is a proud Army wife; currently residing in the MidWest.

For more books and updates:

www.pieceofpiepublishing.com
www.facebook.com/andreahurttauthor
www.Twitter.com/atomicbombshel1
www.Instagram.com/AndreaHurttAuthor
www.Amazon.com/author/andreahurtt